END GAME

An exclusive resort is suffering Net thefts, and Net Force Explorer Megan O'Malley is ready to take the thief down. But the criminal has a plan to put her out of commission—*permanently* . . .

CYBERSPY

A "wearable computer" permits a mysterious hacker access to a person's most private thoughts. It's up to Net Force Explorer David Gray to convince his friends of the danger—before secrets are revealed to unknown spies . . .

SHADOW OF HONOR

Was Net Force Explorer Andy Moore's deceased father a South African war hero or the perpetrator of a massacre? Andy's search for the truth puts every one of his fellow students at risk . . .

PRIVATE LIVES

The Net Force Explorers must delve into the secrets of their commander's life—to prove him innocent of murder . . .

SAFE HOUSE

To save a prominent scientist and his son, the Net Force Explorers embark on a terrifying virtual hunt for their enemies—before it's too late . . .

GAMEPREY

A gamers' convention turns deadly when virtual reality monsters escape their confines—and start tracking down the Net Force Explorers!

TOM CLANCY'S
NET FORCE®

DUEL IDENTITY

CREATED BY

Tom Clancy and **Steve Pieczenik**

Written by Bill McCay

BERKLEY JAM BOOKS, NEW YORK

This is a work of fiction. Names, characters, places, and incidents are either the product of the author's imagination or are used fictitiously, and any resemblance to actual persons, living or dead, business establishments, events, or locales is entirely coincidental.

TOM CLANCY'S NET FORCE: DUEL IDENTITY

A Berkley Jam Book / published by arrangement with
Netco Partners

PRINTING HISTORY
Berkley Jam edition / September 2000

The Penguin Putnam Inc. World Wide Web site address is
http://www.penguinputnam.com

ISBN: 0-425-17634-7

BERKLEY JAM BOOKS®
Berkley Jam Books are published by The Berkley Publishing Group,
a division of Penguin Putnam Inc.,
375 Hudson Street, New York, New York 10014.
BERKLEY JAM and its logo
are trademarks belonging to Penguin Putnam Inc.

PRINTED IN THE UNITED STATES OF AMERICA

10 9 8 7 6 5 4 3 2 1

We'd like to thank the following people, without whom this book would not have been possible: Bill McCay; Martin H. Greenberg, Larry Segriff, Denise Little, and John Helfers at Tekno Books; Mitchell Rubenstein and Laurie Silvers at Hollywood.com, Inc.; Tom Colgan of Penguin Putnam Inc.; Robert Youdelman, Esquire; and Tom Mallon, Esquire; and Robert Gottlieb of the William Morris Agency, agent and friend. We much appreciated the help.

I

The shock of steel against steel quivered up Megan O'Malley's arm as her sword intercepted the saber looping in to slash at her side. As soon as she parried, her opponent's blade leaped away, curving around to threaten her other side.

Megan deflected it again, but she was in trouble—and she knew it. That sword was whistling all around her, and she was scrambling to keep her own weapon in the way. Sooner or later she would mess up, and then . . .

For a wild moment she considered ending her problems with an unexpected karate kick. Bad idea. She knew she had to rely on the saber she held. Funny, even as it kept growing heavier and heavier in her hand, it seemed about as insubstantial as a toothpick when it came to defending her.

Maybe it was time she gave up on defense. . . .

Her opponent's sword swooped high. Desperately Megan raised her sword and threw herself forward to the attack. The "Kiii-yaaah!" she yelled would have been more at home in a karate *dojo*. Anyway, it was cut short—her teeth clicked together as her opponent's saber came down on the top of her head . . . or rather, on the padded top of her fencing mask. At least she had the satisfaction of feeling her own blade slice across her opponent's chest a second later.

Alan Slaney, Megan's instructor at the Capitol Historical Fencing Association, stepped back and removed his mask. He rubbed the front of his fencing jacket where Megan's blow had landed. "What, exactly, would you call that last move?"

His voice was mild enough, but the look in his eyes was one Megan had seen before, usually when she'd just done something really inept.

"A riposte?" she ventured. But even as she spoke, she knew that was the wrong answer. A riposte was a counterattack coming after the defending fencer had parried an opponent's blade.

Megan hadn't even tried to deflect Alan's last stroke. She'd just lashed out. Alan lifted an eyebrow, inviting her to try again.

"Ummm—a stop-thrust?" she tried.

Alan's response was a semi-shrug. "That's a little closer," he said. "But for a stop-thrust to be valid, it has to put a stop to my attack—by landing first. That didn't happen. You didn't have the right of way—the priority— to attack."

"That rule sounds so—so *bogus!*" Megan complained. "I thought this historical swordfighting was supposed to be a martial art, training for the real thing. If this had been an actual duel—"

Alan's voice rode over hers. "If this had been an actual duel, I'd be wincing from a superficial chest cut while trying to wiggle my blade free from your broken skull." He moderated his tone a little. "Fencing conventions aren't rules. They recognize certain realities—basic principles. And the most basic principle of all is that you don't go launching an attack until you've neutralized the danger from your opponent's blade. Otherwise, a better swordsman will take a bite out of you." He grinned. "Two good swordfighters could end up killing each other."

Megan could understand the logic, but she feared her expression was still mutinous.

"Hey, you've had some serious martial arts training," Alan said. "Fencing isn't that different from what you learn in a *dojo*. Rule number one is to be responsible. You didn't go out picking fights after your first few months' worth of karate lessons, did you?"

"No," Megan admitted. "Not that I wasn't tempted."

Alan laughed. "Get out of that mask. We'll go for regular exercises now."

Megan removed her mask, fluffing her damp, dark hair matted down by the protective gear and sweat. She didn't mind sweating—it just meant her muscles were working. And nothing—not even an all-weapons fencing mask—had ever really tamed her mop of curls. Megan grinned at Alan, an automatic response to his sunny disposition.

She glanced around the salle, a large, airy room lined with mirrors along all four walls. Scattered throughout the space, students practiced with each other or worked under the tutelage of instructors. She noticed one student, another newcomer to the salle, slumped forward trying to massage some life into his upper thighs. Those were the muscles that paid the heaviest price as new students tried to adjust to the basic fencing positions. She was lucky. Her extensive martial arts training had kept her from getting too sore. She bounced back pretty well, even after an intense workout like the one she'd just been through. This guy was older—balding and paunchy. His white fencing gear made him look like the Pillsbury Dough Boy. Moments before, Alan had critiqued this guy's shortcomings in much tougher language than he'd used on Megan.

"Let's hit the couches," Alan said.

With a final flip of her hair, Megan ignored the jealous glare of the balding man. *Hey,* she thought, *if you've got it, use it. And if you use it, you might just keep it.* She followed Alan to the rear of the salle, to another room where the computer-link couches stood in a row in front of more traditional training aids for the beginning fencer.

Two of the couches were already occupied. Students reclined on them, eyes closed, faces tight with concentration, the muscles in their arms and legs twitching hard. In the year 2025, virtual learning wasn't unusual. But that much movement on the couch was. Normally, computer couches suppressed most motion on the part of users.

When Megan had first seen the twitching figures, she'd thought something had gone wrong with the salle's computer. Alan had explained that these computer-link couches were specially designed. All couches that allowed people to connect into the Net ran a carefully controlled trickle current into their users to keep their muscles working. Otherwise, everybody, even kids, would end up creaking around when they got up after prolonged Net linkage. The trickle current kept circulation going, kept muscles toned, and kept people who used the Net a lot from turning into couch potatoes.

The couches at the salle carried this toning feature even further. They targeted muscle groups to trigger, so that while students ran through their virtual exercises, they would actually gain strength and the "muscle memory" of the moves they practiced virtually. Megan had been assured the process was perfectly safe, even if the students looked a bit like they were being electrocuted.

Alan was always meticulous about checking the circuitry of each couch before entrusting a student to the machinery. "I'm going to program this so you'll practice the conventional exercises—meeting an attack, parrying, and then the riposte—preferably without adding any on karate yells," he added with a grin.

Megan leaned back onto the yielding material of the couch, closing her eyes. She could still hear Alan talking as the receptors on the couch synched in to the circuitry implanted beneath her skin. "You have an impressive raw talent," Alan said. "But with saber especially, you have to feel the moves right down to your nerves—or so an old fencing master once told me. This virtual practice will give you the moves without working up a sweat, but it's all wasted if you don't pay attention to the thinking behind the moves. You're not a sword-fighting robot—you've got to focus on what the exercises teach you."

Megan's eyes opened, and she was in a virtual copy of the salle's mirrored main space, empty now except for a faceless opponent whose saber began sweeping into that deadly figure-eight pattern. The blade swept close, and automatically her wrist twisted, her blade moving to intercept. . . .

• • •

Leif Anderson stomped into his parents' Manhattan penthouse apartment. Given his present lousy mood, maybe it was just as well the place was empty. Dad was at the office, Mom was lunching late with some old ballet friends, and the cleaning lady was off. He could be as grumpy as he liked, and no one would see.

He dumped his school stuff on the kitchen table and glared down at Park Avenue below while taking swigs of soda right out of the gel-pack. Mom would have gotten on his case to use a glass.

Leif decided it *wasn't* a good thing that no one else was at home. A heaping helping of attitude was no fun if there wasn't anyone to dump it on.

The empty gel-pack in his hand crunched in his grip. Leif wished it was Andy Moore's neck. Andy was the only person he knew who would have set up the prank that had humiliated Leif today.

Last night, just as Leif had put the finishing touches on his report on *Moby Dick*, Andy'd paid a virtual visit from Washington, D.C. The boys had hung around in Leif's virtual workspace, shooting the breeze. Leif had talked about the college-level English course he was taking this summer. And, he remembered, he had mentioned what a babe the instructor was. Krista Mayhew was working on her doctorate at Columbia University, and she made extra money teaching summer sessions at Leif's school. She was tall, smart, slim, and stunning, with blue eyes, short brunette hair, and an athletic figure. Leif'd had half a crush on her from the moment she'd walked into the classroom. Undoubtedly, he'd been just a bit too fixated on the subject of her appearance as he described her to Andy.

The icon representing Leif's report had been out in the open while he'd blathered away. He'd even saved it to a datascrip while Andy had been there. Man, what had he been thinking? Whatever he'd been thinking, it hadn't been good enough. He'd handed Andy an opportunity on a plate—and Andy had used it.

Leif had no premonition of disaster as he turned in his report to Ms. Mayhew. After all, *Moby Dick* had been dissected by generations of students. Leif had had plenty of material to draw on when he wrote his report. He knew it was at least comfortably in the ballpark, and it might even be a home run. He'd done his best, and he thought it showed.

That day, as always, Krista had taken the datascrips from her students one at a time at the beginning of class. As she got each report, she'd inserted it into an old-fashioned laptop computer. Then she opened each file and read a bit of it quickly—something to do with getting a taste of the work her students were doing while she initialized the grading program she used.

After Leif had handed his work in, he'd watched his teacher pull it up on the screen. He had expected to see the first couple of paragraphs of his report swim into view on the computer's display. Instead, an animated hologram appeared—a parade of tiny brunette glamour girls that all bore an alarming resemblance to his teacher, sashaying past on the monitor like a Las Vegas chorus line. Each girl held a small sign, or poster, in front of her, which was just as well, since the girls didn't seem to be wearing anything else. Besides keeping the display rating down to a PG-13 level, the signs carried letters, spaces, or marks. Moving along the line, you could read words—Leif's report, right down to the punctuation.

Ms. Mayhew gave him a glacial look. "I can't grade this on content without reading it. That is apparently going to take rather more effort than I had anticipated.

For presentation, though, I think a definite F is merited here."

Leif had seethed in silence as he realized who had pulled this on him, and his fury had only grown throughout the day and on the way home. Andy could be obnoxious enough at the best of times. But every once in a while, he'd declare what he called "guerrilla class warfare." The purpose, he claimed, was "to keep rich kids from thinking they owned the world."

Since Leif was one of the richer kids Andy knew, he often found himself the victim of his friend's finest pranks. It hadn't helped to imagine Andy sitting safely some two hundred miles away, laughing his head off at the thought of Leif's predicament.

With an abrupt movement Leif tossed his gel-pack into the recycling bin and headed for his room. There was only one way he could work off the mood enveloping him. Leif stripped off his shirt, tossing it on the bed, and sank onto his computer-link couch. He winced his way through the process of linking in.

After being unlucky enough, a bit back, to suffer severe trauma to the nerves around his implants, Leif now found himself extremely sensitive to the process of getting onto the Net. What other people felt as a blink, he experienced as a surge of static and a shooting pain to the brain. And that was under the best of circumstances. He'd been meaning to recalibrate the receptors on his couch lately, but what with summer school and his other activities, he just hadn't found the time. That meant his transition right now was worse than usual. His head felt as if somebody had started a big fat fire right between his ears.

As Leif opened his eyes to the virtual gymnasium around him, his vision was blurred, his eyes actually watering with the pain. *Some distraction this is turning out to be,* he thought sourly. He smoothed his hand over the wire mesh surface on the heavy fencing jacket he wore, then automatically reached behind his back to make sure that the wire for the electrical scoring apparatus was unreeling smoothly. There were newer and better technologies available nowadays for determining which fencer had scored first, but fencing circles tended to be conservative. Electrical scoring for saber bouts was only about fifty years old.

The scene swam into focus, hushed spectators leaning forward on the tiered seats. Leif hadn't taken much trouble with them. They were just background programming, something to get Leif used to the audiences at the actual fencing tournaments where he competed.

But the *piste*, the two-meter by eighteen-meter strip where the fencing bout would take place, was crystal clear. So was the virtual construct that would be Leif's opponent.

"Computer," Leif ordered, "skill level random. No mask. Face . . . Andy Moore." The wire mask hiding his opponent's features vanished to revel Andy's smirking face. This was going to feel *good.* . . .

"*En garde,*" Leif snapped, dropping into the more aggressive of the two guard positions for saber. His sword hand was at chest-level, his arm slightly bent at the elbow, his blade aiming for the virtual Andy's eyes. Leif's other hand hung loosely a few inches from his hip. It was almost a gunslinger's pose.

His opponent, the faux Andy, took the more conservative position, his sword hand at hip level, his blade standing up and out to defend the right side of his torso.

Okay, Leif thought. That still leaves him open for a head or chest cut.

Leif advanced in two rapid steps, feinting with his blade, as the virtual Andy retreated. Footwork was the name of the game in saber fencing, or "gaining the distance," as *sabreurs* called it. Since the sword arm was a target and cuts could come from all sorts of angles, fencers wanted as much room as possible to prepare a parry. The two opponents moved back and forth, testing each other, each trying to confuse the other as to how much space was actually between them.

Then Leif closed the distance, pushing off strongly on his left leg in a running leap, flying at his opponent like an arrow, which is what this move was called in French—the *fleche*. As Leif moved, his rear leg swung forward, and, as his left foot hit the ground again, so did his blow.

The flat of Leif's blade tapped the false Andy on the top of his head. Leif grinned like a wolf at his opponent. At first he'd been tempted to hit hard, to land some blows that would leave bruises the next morning if his opponent were real and the match actual rather than virtual. But Leif's competitive training asserted itself as soon as he faced off. Besides, this was all simulation. He wouldn't be hurting Andy, just swatting at a construct.

Nevertheless, Andy's image grimaced and fell back again. The fencers chased back and forth, each looking for an advantage, and Leif flicked out his blade with fingers and wrist, catching Andy's blade, beating it aside as Leif sliced his adversary on the cheek with the back of his blade. The imitation Andy didn't bleed, but he looked unhappy. Leif came in again, feinting a cut to Andy's head. The simulacrum made the standard defensive move, a parry that brought his blade parallel to the floor and about a foot from his head. Leif immediately abandoned his feint, whipping his blade like lightning to catch the fake Andy on the forearm.

Now the simulacrum launched an attack of his own, slicing his blade in at Leif's left side. Leif shifted his wrist outward while moving his sword across his body, raising the blade almost in a vertical line. The moment he'd parried, his sword leaped forward, the movement all in his fingers—*tap-tap-tap!* He caught his opponent on the forearm, on the shoulder, and on the head.

Not bad for a single extension, Leif thought.

The stand-in Andy looked really angry now, moving fast and going for a head cut. Leif brought his own blade up, and responded with an instant riposte, a swat of the wrist that smacked the flat of his blade against the simulacrum's chest.

His fencing coach would be pleased. Each move Leif made was precise and as quick as lightning—surgical strikes against an ever-more-desperate opponent.

The Andy-faced fencer tried a wide slash. Leif parried and closed in a lunge, flicking out to touch with the point of his blade. "That does it for you," he told the construct.

Sudden applause nearly jarred him into dropping his saber. Leif turned—to find the real Andy Moore, or at least his virtual self, clapping wildly. Good manners would normally keep a person from barging into someone else's virtual setup—not to mention security programs designed to keep out intruders.

But neither manners nor basic firewalls were likely to stop old Andy.

"I came to apologize," Andy said. "But after seeing you cut me up like that—"

Suddenly Leif's lanky blond friend was flanked by a line of virtual cuties, each apparently unclad girl holding a placard. Taken together, they spelled out GO LEIF!

But then the naked ladies and their message pretty much disappeared in the red haze that filled Leif's vision. Blade extended, he charged after Andy, who ducked, dodged, and then simply disappeared from the sim, although his aggravating chuckles still filled the gym.

Leif walked back to face the construct Andy, his face red from fury, exertion . . . and embarrassment. He'd completely lost it while chasing his annoying friend. Not only had he lost his concentration, he'd been chopping as if his saber were a meat cleaver.

He brought his blade up in a quick salute. "*En garde*," he said. "It appears I've got a little more to work off with you."

2

Leif popped into the big, bare virtual meeting room with only a twinge from his temples.

Very nice, he thought. Recalibrating the lasers on his computer-link couch had paid off. He looked around the government-issue meeting space. The crowd of kids assembled for the monthly national meeting of the Net Force Explorers looked sparser than usual. Well, it *was* summer, and a lot of kids spent their time doing interesting things in the real world instead of venturing into cyberspace.

But not Leif—right now the real world around him was too darned hot. New York was going through one of its periodic summer heat waves. Dad was working on some massive deal that required his physical presence round the clock at the office, while Mom was chairing a big charity event that kept her occupied and away from home more often than not. For Leif, the decision to leave his body in air-conditioned comfort back in the penthouse while seeing his D.C. friends was a no-brainer.

He'd even mostly gotten over his anger with Andy Moore—although his second bout with the make-believe Andy had been a lot more intense than the first one. No neat little taps for scoring purposes that time. But the virtual carnage served him well. Leif was feeling sufficiently magnanimous not to go for Andy's throat when the blond boy popped into existence not too far away.

"Hey, D'Artagnan," Andy greeted Leif with a smirk. "How's school?"

"Don't push it, Moore."

"You have to admit it was funny," Andy said.

"Ask me in six months," Leif said. "Right now, no, I'm not laughing."

David Gray joined them—as usual, the crew was homing in on Leif's head of blazing red hair. "Thanks for your warning," David said to Leif. "I checked my files after a visit from the schlock-meister here, and ended up editing topless dancers out of the telemetry package from my reproduction of the *Galileo* space probe."

"You told?" Andy flashed a look of betrayal at Leif, quickly followed by outrage as he turned to David. "And they *weren't* topless! Each figure stays respectably behind her letter card"—he smiled slyly—"unless somebody found a way to erase the cards."

"You'd better not try slipping any nudie munchkins into *my* system, Moore," Maj Greene entered the conversation with her usual volume and energy. "*I* wouldn't be satisfied with just trashing you in veeyar."

Heads began turning at the sound of her raised voice.

Andy held up his hands. "They're not nude," he said feebly. "Just . . . cute."

"My lit instructor didn't think they were cute," Leif told him. "Trust me on that one."

"What's all the hubbub?" Megan O'Malley asked as she synched in.

As David explained, she shook her head. "You guys just don't know how to spend your summers."

"And you do?" Maj challenged. "Running around waving a sword?"

"Nothing wrong with that," Leif quickly put in. "Although why you'd want to learn a bunch of obsolete mumbo-jumbo—"

"I'll bet I've learned more about the *why* of things studying historical fencing that you ever heard of in your competitive fencing bouts, Mr. Junior Champion," Megan shot back. "My instructor is really into the history of the blade. In fact, Alan is into history in general. He's a charter member of the *Fin de Siècle* SIG in the local AHSO chapter."

"What?" Maj demanded. "What kind of acronym is that? Does the group check out the historical significance of Chinese food?"

"The letters stand for Amalgamated Historical Simulation Organizations," David said. "SIG means Special Interest Group, right?"

Matt Hunter, another member of the group, came up to join them, followed by P.J. Farris.

"Aren't they the guys who go around playing knights in shining armor?" P.J. asked.

"More than that," David replied. "They've extended their interests to all the various eras of history. Each time period and geographical area is covered by a SIG—a Special Interest Group."

Matt Hunter nodded. "*Fin de Siècle* is the SIG for the turn of the century from the eighteen-nineties into the nineteen-hundreds."

Matt ought to know, Leif thought. His friend was into history in a big way. "Good name for it—*the end of the era*," Leif said, translating the phrase from the French into English.

"Alan invited me to come and check out their next meeting," Megan went on. "He made it sound like a lot of fun."

"My dad is always talking about our great Texas history," P.J. said. His father was a senator for the Lone Star State. "Not much swordplay down our way, though, unless you count bowie knives. Bows, arrows, fists, and guns were pretty much the weapons of choice in the bad old days in Texas."

"Alan wouldn't think much of Texas, then," Megan said. "He's fondest of times where swashbuckling heroes performed great deeds of daring with daggers drawn, not to mention sabers, rapiers, and any other kind of edged weapon you can think of."

Leif rolled his eyes. "This Slaney guy sounds like he thinks he's God's gift to fencing, and maybe history, as well."

"Not to mention God's gift to women," Andy added, nodding toward Megan. She seemed very up about her summer activities, her upcoming visit with the *Fin de Siècle* SIG . . . and Alan Slaney in general.

Leif cut into her earnest attempts to recruit some friends to go along with her. "All right. What's the Net address for this tea party?"

Megan glanced over at him. "It's not a veeyar thing," she said. "These guys are very old-fashioned. They meet in the flesh."

A stir in the crowd and a turning of heads showed that the Net Force Explorers meeting was finally starting. That would cut off any more discussion until after business was taken care of.

Leif shrugged. It looked as if he wasn't going to get to check out this Slaney person. He wasn't coming down all the way from New York to check out the possible competition from a guy who *might* want to go out with Megan.

After all, Leif wasn't going out with her, either.

Megan stood in front of the building, glancing from the number over the glass doors to the address Alan Slaney had written down for her. She'd expected the *Fin de Siècle* SIG to meet in a restaurant, or maybe in somebody's home—the old-fashioned houses around Dupont Circle would have been perfect. Instead, she found herself outside a large downtown office building. At least, it would have been an office building twenty years ago. Nowadays, the building provided more space for computers and servers than for actual workers.

Maj Green came out through the revolving doors. "This definitely is the place," she reported. "Maybe we should wait in the lobby. It's about twenty degrees cooler than the air out here."

"I guess they keep the place well air-conditioned for the computers," Megan said. "If you want to stay inside, that's okay with me. But I think one of us should be out here—that's where we said we'd meet."

Another girl passed them, carrying a long, very full garment bag inside.

"That's the fifth person I've seen with one of those things," Megan said. "What are they for?"

"Costumes," Maj told her. "I almost couldn't get into

the ladies' room with all the people changing in there. I sat and watched them for a minute. Getting dressed in those days must have been a big deal. Too many layers and no zippers. I learned a bit about turn-of-the-century clothes while I was there. They had to be awful hot in a Washington summer." She waggled her fingers. "And they had lots of hooks and buttons."

P.J. Farris hopped out of a cab and gave the building a long once-over. "Well, it is old-fashioned, but it's still about sixty years ahead of the times for these AHSO people."

"They needed a large-sized meeting place, and Alan was able to arrange this with his boss," Megan explained.

Andy came walking from the direction of the nearest Metro station with David. Obviously, he'd heard what Megan had said. "Your pal Alan works here?" Andy said. "Doing what?"

"Computer maintenance." The words felt awkward on Megan's tongue.

"Maintenance? On those sealed boxes they keep in here?" Andy hooted. "That means dusting. The guy's a glorified janitor!"

Maj and P.J. joined Andy's laughter. Megan could feel her face going stiff as she looked over at David.

He shrugged. "It's not the greatest job in the world."

"Alan says it pays the rent," Megan defended her friend, "and gives him time to do the things he wants to do."

"Like fooling around with swords and the good old days," Maj snorted.

"He says it was a simpler, more beautiful time," Megan said.

David shook his head. His dark brown skin gleamed

in the light. "Simpler, yes. As for beautiful, I don't think so. Things sure were a lot simpler for folks who were my color," he pointed out. "There were only a few jobs we were allowed to do. Picking cotton, cleaning houses, shining shoes—"

"And there were only a couple of states where women were allowed to vote," Maj put in.

"I was just repeating Alan's opinion. You don't have to convince me how much better things are today. What do you say we just check out what these people are doing?" Megan said. "Alan seemed really eager about tonight's meeting."

Megan and her friends entered the building, following the growing crowd heading to the meeting room. Megan couldn't believe her eyes as they entered. A good quarter of the people in the room were dressed in period costumes. One guy came by in a dapper-looking suit, his derby tucked under one arm as he swung an agate-topped cane in the other. Then they passed a girl wearing a hobble skirt so tight around the ankles she could hardly walk, along with a jacket that ended at her waist, and a hat wider than a pizza crowned with all sorts of iridescent feathers.

"I'll bet that hemline raised people's blood pressure back when," David said with a smile.

"You can't see anything!" Andy complained.

"In those days a glimpse of stocking was hot stuff," David replied. "Too bad Matt's not around. He'd have enjoyed this, I think."

"I think he'll get by, vacationing with his family," P.J. laughed, then stared. "Check *this* one out."

"*This*" turned out to be a guy in a red uniform covered in gold braid, with a fore-and-aft hat, a gold-encrusted

sash . . . and a sword with a gold hilt in an ornate scabbard.

"Either he rules half a continent, or he's the doorman
for a *very* exclusive hotel," P.J. said.

"Nice sword," Maj muttered, turning to Megan.
"Please, tell me this isn't your friend."

"No," Megan was happy to answer. "There he is."

Alan stepped out on a small stage, dressed in everyday
jeans and a polo shirt. "Glad to see you could all make
it," he told the crowd, with a special grin at the guy in
the general's rig. "Especially you, Chauncey."

"Think nothing of it, old boy," the guy in the glittering uniform replied with a condescending wave of his
fawn-colored glove.

Except for the costumes and the slightly more informal tone, the business part of the meeting wasn't all that
different from the Net Force Explorers gathering a few
days earlier. In fact, Alan's final announcement was
more high-tech than historical.

"I'm happy to say that Latvinia is up and running,"
Alan told them.

"Was she sick?" Andy Moore cracked—a little too
loudly, Megan realized.

Alan pretended not to notice. "For almost a year, people have been talking about a virtual reality setup that
would let us simulate life in our chosen era. Latvinia
gives us an entire kingdom—even though it's a small
one—with plenty of opportunities for adventures. It's
based on some of the vest-pocket monarchies created in
period novels like *The Prisoner of Zenda*, the *Graustark*
stories, and Edgar Rice Burroughs's *The Mad King*."

"Sounds like you'd have to be insane to get involved
with this," Maj commented.

The response from the rest of the crowd—the non-

Net Force Explorers—was much more enthusiastic.

"What happens now?" asked the girl in the hobble skirt.

"Beta-testing," Alan replied. "The sim and all the non-playing characters are ready to go. If you're interested in visiting Latvinia, check with me, get a character profile, and fill it out. We'll run it through the computer, and you'll be in." He seemed to be looking straight at Megan as he said, "This is an open invitation. I hope we get a good response."

"Excuse me," an accented voice called out. Megan glanced over to recognize a young foreign guy from her historical fencing classes. "This invitation—it is for all of us? Even those who do not belong to this organization?"

"Let me introduce Sergei Chernevsky, the son of the Russian ambassador," Alan said. "I took the liberty tonight of inviting Sergei and several other promising fencers from the historical swordplay class I teach." He grinned. "After all, what would Latvinia be without flashing blades? For that we need swordsmen—and swordswomen."

"Oh, brother," Andy said.

"From the determined look on Megan's face," David said, "I'd cut that down to a simple—'Uh-oh!' "

Leif scowled at the holographic connection to Washington. "How can you say that?" he demanded.

"It's a pretty simple two-letter word," David Gray replied. "N-O. No."

Leif shook his head as he looked at his friend's face.

"I don't see what the problem is," David added. "Maj and Andy turned Megan down flat. P.J. wants to play cowboys and Cossacks, or whatever. Just because you volunteered to join in on this beta-testing jaunt doesn't mean I have to come along."

"I wish—" Leif began.

David cut him off. "Have you read any of the books this mythical kingdom is supposedly based on?"

"Not while I was preparing for my lit class final," Leif replied. "I had to make a good grade on it after Andy sabotaged that written report."

"Well, I read them. I found only one character who was African-American—a train porter who talked in the vilest dialect you could imagine."

"Colonial French?" Leif suggested.

"Cornpone English," David corrected. "I am *not* going to run around in veeyar crying, 'Lawdy, lawdy!' "

"I'd just feel a lot better if we had someone along who knew down to the smallest detail how these sims worked," Leif said. "It's one thing to buy into a commercial game world, but this Slaney guy programmed Latvinia by himself."

"And you wouldn't even be going in at all except 'this Slaney guy' all but offered Megan a personal invitation." David shook his head. "Frankly, compared to the dress-up brigade I saw at that meeting, he seemed like a tower of normality . . . and a pretty nice guy. If Megan wants to go play in his make-believe country, why don't you let her, instead of horning in—and trying to drag me along?"

"David, I need the favor," Leif finally said. "I'll owe you one, big-time. Just come in and check the place out. If you really hate your character, I'll get you out immediately."

David just looked at him, his eyebrows rising. "And how will you do that?" he asked.

"The quickest exit possible from a sim," Leif responded with a laugh. "I'll kill you—you have my personal guarantee."

"Anybody know where my book on poisons is?" Megan's father asked as he rooted around in the living room. "It's not on the bookshelf in its usual place." Megan glanced over to where her father had been working. A thick tome on Norse mythology had several pieces of paper stuck in it marking various pages, while beside it lay something titled *Great Teen Detectives of the Twentieth Century*. She was almost afraid to ask what writing project Dad had embarked on now.

"Maybe Mom has it?" Megan suggested. "I just hope Sean hasn't picked it up. It's his turn to cook next week."

Ordinarily, she'd help her father search for the escaped book, but one look at the clock just now had stopped her from volunteering. Tonight was the night that she, David, Leif, and P.J. were entering Latvinia for the first time.

Alan had okayed the idea of Megan going in with her friends, so long as they submitted character profiles just like everyone else. She'd spent a day filling in the long form that had appeared in her virtmail box, answering questions about her interests and abilities. David had almost pulled out again, but she and Leif had nagged him back into line.

More annoying had been Alan's insistence on keeping the results of those forms secret.

"You'll discover your character when you go in," he told her. "Everybody gets a full background as they get started. This isn't some commercial sim where you can pick and choose your character. I've got a kingdom to run here, and I won't be able to do it if everybody starts pestering me about changes."

Pestering Alan to tell her more hadn't worked, either. He'd kept her so busy in fencing class she scarcely had breath to ask questions.

So, as she settled into the computer-link couch in her room, Megan still had no idea what she was getting into. When she appeared in Latvinia, she could be a count-ess—or a scullery maid.

No sense worrying about it now, she told herself as the couch receptors began to synch in with her implanted circuits. She closed her eyes, thinking about the pile of dishes she'd helped clean after dinner tonight. She hoped she wouldn't be doing the same job in veeyar.

I'll never live it down with the guys if this blows up in my face, Megan thought.

She opened her eyes—and a loud explosion almost sent her tumbling to the floor!

3

Megan's eyes shot open as she was nearly flung from the seat of an old-fashioned vehicle that looked more like a boat than an automobile. She grabbed hold of the steering wheel as she took in the scenery—stark gray mountains surrounding a winding dirt road.

"Mind being a little more careful with the starting switch so that doesn't happen again?" Leif's annoyed voice came from the front of the car.

Megan glanced over the hood of the car—and blinked. Leif had changed. He looked several years older and sported a blazing red, close-cropped beard. He also wore a sturdy cap made of something like canvas, and a matching coat—a motoring coat. The name seemed to pop into her mind. A pair of leather and glass goggles was pushed up on his forehead.

Leif scowled down at something below the car's

radiator as he wiped sweat off his face. "That backfire threw the starter handle back against my cranking." He rubbed his arm, giving her a dubious look. "I could have broken something. You *do* know how to drive one of these things?"

"Of course," Megan snapped, looking over the dials and contraptions around the driver's seat. *That's* the starter, a little voice seemed to whisper in her ear as her eyes landed on a fluted brass button down on the floor.

Her hands moved as if they had a mind of their own to a metal gizmo in the center of the mahogany steering wheel. They made a minute adjustment on a metal lever. Meanwhile, Leif put his back into turning the crank— again, and yet again. A low rumble sounded from deep in the car, followed by a sputter from the engine as Megan hit the ignition. She worked the throttle, giving the engine some gas. The whole car shook as the engine roared. Another quick adjustment, and the noise changed to a mechanical purr.

"Good." Leif disengaged the crank and climbed up into the car.

A little belatedly Megan realized that she was sitting in what she would consider the passenger seat of a modern car—but the wheel was on her side.

"I still think we should have taken horses," P.J. Farris's voice came from the backseat.

Megan looked back as she shifted to the passenger's seat, and Leif got behind the wheel. P.J. also looked older and deeply tanned. He wore a motoring coat and a wide-brimmed Stetson sombrero. Beside him, sitting bolt upright with his arms folded, was David. He wore a similar coat—and a turban. A close-trimmed goatee framed his lips.

Even as she looked at them, a surge of information seemed to flood Megan's brain. It was almost like double vision, seeing her friends grown and strange—with different names and histories. P.J., for instance, was Bronco Jack Farris, of the Bear Creek Farrises, a rich ranching family. His parents had sent him on a tour of Europe to pick up a little old-world polish.

David was Menelik of Gondar, a prince of Abyssinia. Megan knew that was the old-time name for Ethiopia. In 1880 Abyssinia had successfully repelled an invasion aimed at turning the country into an Italian colony. Menelik was traveling to discover the benefits of European technology—and to assess the dangers of imperialist hostility.

Megan glanced over at Leif—but now he was also Albrecht von Hengist, a Scandinavian noblemen. A down-on-his-luck nobleman, Megan suspected, if he had to make a living escorting such an odd gathering of tourists.

And she herself was Marguerite O'Malley, of the New York O'Malleys. Her father had been a Union general in the Civil War, and her family had prospered in the postwar boom times. She was the second generation of the family to enjoy wealth and power, even if the big Society families didn't accept them. After four years in a girl's college, she'd gotten the chance to travel . . . a chance for adventure.

Oh, she knew she was really Megan O'Malley, whose parents were freelance writers, and that her real home was back in Washington, D.C., in 2025. But she also "knew" that here it was the spring of 1903, and that she and her fellow travelers were at the border of the small kingdom of Latvinia.

Alan certainly managed to pump a lot of information into his simulation—and into the role-players' heads. She glanced over at Leif/Albrecht, who continued to scowl as he steered the touring car.

"Cantankerous hunk of junk," he muttered. "Does a sim have to be this historical?"

David, on the other hand, patted the varnished coach-work fondly. "This, my friend, is a 1901 Mercedes Simplex—named after Mercedes, the daughter of Emil Jellinek, the man who pushed through the design of the car."

"A historical junk-pile," Leif grumbled.

"Get a horse!" P.J. cried.

"You'd need forty of them to match the output of this engine," David continued to defend their vehicle. "Given the era, this is something of a speed machine."

"Not on these roads," Leif said as they bounced over ruts in the hard dirt.

"Oh, look!" Megan pointed to a peak overlooking the road. Three horsemen seemed almost to be posing against the afternoon sky. They were dressed in brightly colored woolen jackets—and each had a long-barreled rifle strapped across his shoulder.

"The first *Graustark* novel had a couple of guys like that," David said. "A bit of local color. Although they looked like bandits, they were actually border guards."

The Mercedes chugged upward around the side of the mountain, then swung downward into a dip in the road—and a welcome patch of shade cast by tall bushes.

But the road ahead was now blocked by the three picturesque "border guards," who were unlimbering their rifles, while more characters in colorful local dress came out of the bushes, waving clubs.

"Looks like this sim *is* different from the old books," Megan said. "They really *are* bandits!"

"Out of the car!" Leif ordered as he pulled the car over. "Otherwise, we'll be sitting ducks. Er—Jack—" He stumbled over P.J.'s player name. "Deal with those fellows on horseback blocking our way. David, er, Menelik, you cover him. I'll protect Miss O'Malley."

Two guys with clubs were charging up as he leaped from behind the wheel, his hand dropping to the hilt of his saber.

Lucky I stowed it right by the seat, he thought, pulling the blade free. "Meg . . . Miss Marguerite . . . stay back!"

He went into the *en garde* position, a little hampered by his heavy coat. This wasn't exactly like a fencing competition. The saber he held was a real weapon, somewhat heavier than he was used to. And, of course, it wasn't blunted or button-tipped. It would cut any of the club-toting bandits who came too close.

Then a cannon seemed to go off by his left ear. Leif half-turned to see Megan daintily aiming a small gold and ivory revolver.

"What are you do—" Leif began.

That was when the robber's club came down on his shoulder. It wasn't a huge stick—somewhere between a cane and a baseball bat in size, not that Leif was in any shape to worry about it. But it was enough to take Leif out of the fight. His vision dissolved in a bright-red nova of pain as he sank to one knee, struggling to hold onto his sword and his consciousness.

Megan aimed carefully, pulled the trigger, and drilled the club-wielder in the shoulder. He staggered back, joining his friend that she'd shot in the thigh on the

ground. While covering them, Megan glanced around to
see how the fight was going.

"YEEEEE-HAAAA!" P.J. stood on the backseat of
the Mercedes, leveling a pair of Army Colt pistols. The
six-shooters roared, taking out two of the mounted bandits before they'd even aimed their rifles. The third
mounted bandit abruptly crouched low in the saddle,
urging his horse into a retreat.

But even as P.J. fired, one of the brigands was rushing
at him from the side, waving a club that looked like a
young tree trunk. David stepped into his way, uncer-
tainly hefting a curved scimitar.

I hope he knows how to use it, Megan thought. *Just
as I suddenly knew how to use this particular model of
gun.*

The bandit swung, and David backpedaled, bumping
into the side of the Mercedes. Megan tried to aim, but
couldn't get a clear shot. Desperately David took a two-
handed grip on his sword as the brigand raised his club
again. David whipped the scimitar around was if it were
a baseball bat . . . and got more results than he'd ever
anticipated.

The steel blade swept right through the robber's forearm, slicing across muscle and bone to complete a very
rough amputation. With a high-pitched scream, the bandit staggered back, clutching at the wound.

The rest of the robbers also pulled back momentarily.
Leif and his friends had taken out more than half of the
robber band. The others were clearly wavering between
running away and staging another attack. Megan decided
not to fool around with them. "P.J.! Cover our rear!"

As P.J. turned to stand on the seat facing the remaining bandits, Megan bundled the still-dazed Leif into the
back beside him. Then she jumped behind the wheel,

thankful that the engine was still idling. David jumped into the passenger seat, and Megan tromped on the gas pedal. The Mercedes lurched forward, nearly toppling P.J. from his perch. Even so, a couple of wild shots from his big Army Colts discouraged the bandits from following.

Safely away, Megan glanced at David sitting beside her. His dark face seemed tinged with gray as he obsessively wiped the blade of his scimitar.

"That was just too real. It cut right through—" he began. Then he gulped and shook his head as if to clear the memory away.

Megan thought she understood. Lots of the games and sims she'd played involved zapping or shooting enemies. But commercial sims didn't feature the kind of combat David had gone through. A sword usually *chunk*ed into an opponent's shield or clanged off armor, or protective scales on some sort of mythological monster. Even in virtual reality, people didn't generally experience anything quite like what they'd just witnessed.

"How's Leif—er, the baron—doing?" she asked rather belatedly.

"Could have been worse," P.J. reported while Leif gave a low grunt of pain. "These coats we're wearing are thick, and his shoulder padding managed to break a lot of the impact."

"*Break*—that's a word I really don't want to hear right now," Leif muttered, giving another yelp as P.J. probed where he'd been hit.

"You wouldn't be able to squirm around with that arm if your collarbone were really broken," P.J. announced in his best country-doctor fashion. "At worst, you'll have a beautiful bruise to show for it."

"One thing's sure," Megan said. "I'll do the driving

until you've had a chance to get your wind back. What was our destination supposed to be, anyway?"

"We're heading for Herzen, the capital of Latvinia," Leif said, his voice tight with pain. "It's the one big city there, located in the middle of the kingdom." His breath hissed between his teeth as the car jolted over a pothole. "Which is also where the few decent roads are to be found."

"And how do we get there?" David asked, opening a leather map case.

"This road will take us alongside, then down into the Dubok Valley," Leif replied. "That's where the rail line from Vienna runs into the country. Once we get down into the valley, things should be a little less wild. We should reach the outskirts of Herzen by nightfall."

"Which means we should be moving now, while we have sunlight," Megan said. They jounced along the mountain track until they finally reached a ridgeline that overlooked a valley below. Megan spotted the glint of sunlight off steel rails.

"So, this is the Dubok Valley?"

Leif leaned carefully forward, still favoring his hurt shoulder. "Yes. There should be a fork in the road ahead. Take the path leading downward—and be prepared for a rather steep grade. These roads see more mules and goats than motorcars."

Leif's shifted to a more turn-of-the-century style of talking, Megan thought. *Maybe he's feeling a bit better.*

They continued along the rim of the valley, which was still pretty narrow and rugged. In the distance, however, the lowlands began to spread out. Megan could even make out what seemed to be plowed fields.

Then she saw the train stopped on the tracks far below, and heard the pop of gunfire. About twenty black-clad riders on equally black horses swarmed around a gilded passenger car at the rear of the train. A handful of guards in crimson uniforms and shining brass helmets struggled against the horsemen. Even as Megan watched, the last defender went down.

Several of the black riders swung onto the observation deck at the rear of the coach and went inside it. Seconds later they emerged with a struggling female figure wrapped in a black cloak.

"It seems as though Latvinia has a serious crime problem," Megan commented. "First we encounter a robbery, and now an abduction."

The kidnappers unceremoniously bundled their prisoner onto a horse and began galloping off up the far wall of the valley, where another road twisted out of sight among the trees.

"What's their hurry?" P.J. wondered. "We sure aren't in any position to stop them."

His answer came moments later, when what looked like an army on horseback came pounding along the valley floor.

"They must have come from Herzen," Megan said, gazing down on the charging squadrons. Some of the cavalrymen wore dark green and gray uniforms that matched the rocks and brush of the countryside. Others were obviously ceremonial troops in crimson and gold uniforms. Some even wore gleaming steel breastplates on their chests. All had swords or pistols out as they reached the locomotive, which had crashed into a chopped-down tree.

The soldiers surrounded the stranded train, some dismounting to assist the downed guards. A group of splendidly uniformed officers gathered in a knot by the raided passenger coach. They waved their arms in obvious agitation.

Then one of them must have noticed the Mercedes moving along the road above. Binoculars were trained on the car, and aides began riding to the assembled soldiers. Soon a large detachment of cavalry went veering off to start climbing the valley wall.

"Perhaps we might pull over," Leif suggested. "I'd hate to have this coachwork ruined by a volley of warning shots."

Megan brought the Mercedes to the side of the road as a patrol of light cavalry came pounding up behind them. Each rider was armed with a wicked-looking lance that was taller than she was.

"Ah—good day?" Megan tried in both French and German.

The soldiers surrounded the car, but they simply sat on their horses staring at her.

What was the matter with them? Megan wondered. Hadn't they ever seen a girl before? She checked that her hat was still held in place by her scarf. Was there something wrong with her coat? Had one of those bozos who'd attacked them gotten blood all over it?

Before she could ask what the problem was, the main body of horsemen arrived. Some looked as if they'd just come from a costume shop, in fancy uniforms with an embroidered jacket worn like a cape. The others were heavy cuirassiers, the guys in steel breastplates. Megan saw a familiar face among the caped riders. Sergei Chernevsky grinned and flipped her a salute from the visor of his uniform cap.

Sergei hastily lowered his hand and sat very straight on his saddle as a very dignified-looking old geezer creakily got down off his horse. The large white side-whiskers flanking the older man's face seemed to tremble as he hurried toward the car.

He seized Megan's hand in both of his and pressed a kiss to it. Then he looked up, exclaiming in a shaky voice, "Thank heavens you escaped, Your Majesty!"

4

Megan glanced around at her friends, who all were suffering from a bad case of dropped-jaw syndrome. As was the old geezer, when she looked back at him.

Okay, she thought. *It makes a sort of sense. The sim is based on* The Prisoner of Zenda, *where a guy winds up impersonating royalty. I didn't expect Alan would take it so literally. . . .*

She grinned. Or that he'd give me such a plum role.

"On second glance, forgive me, my dear young lady," the old geezer murmured quietly over her hand. "Now that I've seen your attire and your companions, I realize you can't really be Princess Gwenda. But your resemblance is both astonishing and fortuitous. Please, follow my lead. You can help save my country . . . if you wish."

His eyes were pleading as he looked up.

"Who are you?" Megan asked.

"I'm the Graf von Esbach," the older man replied. "Prime minister of Latvinia."

Megan gave him a solemn nod. "I thank you for your concern, Graf von Esbach," she said in a loud voice. "If these gentlemen hadn't come along at the right moment, those brigands would most surely have abducted me."

Von Esbach looked up with hope in his eyes. "Colonel Vojak, dispatch a troop in pursuit of those would-be kidnappers! I myself will accompany the princess to Herzen with a detachment of Hussars!"

P.J. vaulted from the backseat. "Tell you what, Mr. Graf. Suppose I ride your horse while you ride this here vee-hick-ull?"

Von Esbach bowed. "An excellent idea, Herr—"

"I'm a him," P.J. replied with a grin. "Bronco Jack Farris—of the Bear Creek Farrises." He stepped over to the cavalryman holding von Esbach's mount, took the reins, and swung into the saddle. The horse immediately reared, trying to throw him, but P.J. clung to the saddle as if he were part of the animal. "Mighty spirited piece of horseflesh for an older feller."

"The Graf rode that horse leading the charge that broke the Ostwalder battleline during the last war," the trooper told him.

"You could have told me that before I hopped on," P.J. growled.

The cavalryman gave him a smile. "And miss the Wild West show?"

Leif resumed the driving duties while Von Esbach rode in the back with Megan. Colonel Vojak rode alongside at a little distance. The Graf filled the colonel in on what had really just happened.

"Can you explain this amazing resemblance?"

Megan shrugged as newly implanted memories rose

up. "I have an ancestor who was one of the Wild
Geese—soldiers who fled conquered Ireland and fought
for other lands. He came home with a bride from these
parts that he swore was a lost princess. We all thought
it was just a wild story he made up to impress his drinking buddies."

"Whatever the history, we must count ourselves lucky
that you appeared when you did," von Esbach replied.
"Without Princess Gwenda, Latvinia faces a dire crisis.
The king, your father—" He broke off. "The princess's
father . . . was a great man and a good king. But now he
is on his deathbed, and traitors plan to steal the throne."

"The princess has a cousin, Gray Piotr, Master of
Grauheim," Colonel Vojak said. "He wishes to become
master of all Latvinia."

The prime minister nodded. "Throughout the king's
illness, Piotr has worked to install his creatures in places
of power. Members of the government have resigned, or
suffered . . . accidents."

"Accidents? Bah!" Vojak growled. "Several army
commanders were apparently sharpening their swords,
and then fell on them—backward. At least the King's
Guard stays true."

"The colonel's command," von Esbach explained.
"For the most part, the army, the government, and indeed, the people of Latvinia are loyal. But if the king
should die and his daughter not appear . . ."

Megan nodded. "It would seem as though *she* weren't
loyal. But how could this Piotr fellow get the people
behind him?"

"I can only imagine—and fear," the prime minister
said. "If the princess failed to appear, and then turned
up dead, with proof that the Ostwalders had attacked
her—"

"It would mean war, with every Latvinian marching for vengeance behind brave King Piotr." Colonel Vojak looked as though he wanted to spit. "Not that von Esbach and I need to worry about that. No doubt we'd be already dead."

"But if I arrive in Herzen as the princess, the machinery of the plot grinds to a halt," Megan said.

"Piotr would have to eliminate you—either through assassination or by unmasking you." Vojak stated the situation unflinchingly.

"But we can hope and pray that the true Princess Gwenda would remain alive," Graf von Esbach said.

"Alive—but a prisoner," Megan pointed out. "Where would this Gray Piotr be holding her?"

"Anywhere in his domains," Vojak replied. "Grauheim is the tallest mountain in Latvinia, surrounded by some of our wildest countryside. There are more hunting lodges, old fortresses, and plain robbers' dens than anyone could count."

"Starting now, they'll have to be counted—and checked," Leif spoke up from the front of the car. "Miss O'Malley's appearance buys you some time. But neither the country nor the real princess is safe until she's rescued."

"All too true," Colonel Vojak growled.

As they'd driven along, the valley had widened still farther, turning into rich farmland. Now a large town or small city appeared in the distance, quaint, old-fashioned buildings surrounding an even older medieval wall. Dominating everything for miles around was a castle or palace in the middle of the town. As Megan stared, a red rocket shot up from one of the towers. "We've been spotted." Colonel Vojak turned to Megan with a formal bow. "Are you ready to greet your people, Princess?"

Megan had to push back a sudden surge of stage fright. "As ready as I'll ever be," she answered.

Leif could barely keep his mind on his driving as he aimed the car down the grand boulevard of Herzen. He kept shooting suspicious glances at the cheering crowds all around them. The townsfolk were all waving green, red, and gold flags and shouting their heads off to welcome the "princess."

But Leif, recalling certain events prior to World War I, especially the assassination of Archduke Francis Ferdinand, heir to the Austrian throne, couldn't help but think how easy it would be for someone to burst from that crowd waving a revolver. If that were to happen, Leif was determined to make a good try at running any such assassin down before the fatal shot was fired.

Beside him, David—or Menelik—glanced into the backseat and shook his head.

"How's she doing?" Leif asked in a whisper.

"She's eating it up," his friend replied quietly. "What do you expect? Who wouldn't like riding into town in the back of a fancy car and having everyone treat you as if you're the greatest thing since sliced bread?"

They continued along the wide street until they found themselves at the gates of the castle that dominated the town. Thick oak doors strapped with steel swung inward to admit them, revealing a courtyard with beautiful gardens.

"What do we do now?" Leif heard Megan ask Graf von Esbach.

"I think a visit to the king is on the order of business, first and foremost," the prime minister replied. "And then, perhaps to the throne room. All the nobles of the land will have gathered to welcome their princess back."

Leif brought the Mercedes to a stop, and Megan got out, removing her rather dusty motoring coat. She'd already taken off her hat and scarf while waving to the Latvinian people on the boulevard. Servants came rushing to take care of any needs the "princess" might have. Von Esbach waved them off.

"This way," he said in a low voice, circling around the inner walls of the palace. They entered through a smaller, inconspicuous door. A pair of guards in crimson and gold stood at attention.

Trailing along behind the prime minister and Megan, Leif, David, and P.J. marched through a maze of corridors. Leif wondered if the royal architect had been drinking when he designed the castle, or if the wandering halls were a security measure to confuse attackers. They certainly confused him. Here and there portraits and tapestries brought bits of color to ancient graystone walls.

"I keep expecting to see Dracula's brother-in-law come popping out of the shadows," P.J. whispered.

"Let's concentrate on the real-life dangers," Leif whispered back.

"Odds are that the conspirators know that Megan has arrived by now," David said, taking on the situation logically. "We'll probably have a short breathing period while they decide what they're going to do."

Provided nobody loses it and tries to take out this new Princess Gwenda before she's really in play, a suspicious voice muttered in the back of Leif's head.

They seemed to zigzag back and forth for a bit, then climbed a circular staircase into one of the castle towers. This part of the castle had been modernized, and the hallways began to show a few creature comforts—thick carpets on the stone floors and even more tapestries.

Looks like someone might actually live here, Leif thought. They arrived at a guarded door. Only Megan and von Esbach went through.

The boys stood around for a bit.

Some minutes later, the Graf and Megan returned. Leif noticed that Megan looked very serious. "The king doesn't actually look like your father, does he?" he asked in a low voice as they proceeded down the corridor.

"No." Megan shook her head. "That would be way too weird. The king is in a coma, so the Graf used our visiting time to prepare me for the people I'll meet in the throne room."

A different—and equally confusing—route brought them down to ground level. This was obviously the public part of the palace. Everything was done up in grand style, from the paintings on the wall to the furniture to the guards standing stiffly at attention.

At last they reached a huge pair of double doors that not only had guards but a pair of uniformed flunkies in knee-breeches and powdered wigs. They'd have looked more at home as doormen for George Washington than for a twentieth-century kingdom. At the first sight of von Esbach and Megan, they leaped into action, opening the doors.

Megan took a deep breath. "Wish me luck," she whispered.

Leif didn't say anything—not out loud. But a voice in his head jeered, *You'll need it.*

Megan swept through the door on the Graf von Esbach's arm, doing her best not to gawk at Latvinia's throne room. It wasn't as large as the virtual space used to house Net Force Explorer meetings—not quite. But the crowd of waiting nobles made up in color what they lacked in numbers.

I always thought the turn of the century was a pretty conservative time, Megan thought as she took in the assembled throng. *Guess I was wrong.*

The wild fashions of the *Fin de Siècle* SIG should have warned her. Here, in veeyar, the costumes were even more extreme. Most of the males were in some sort of uniform, with an apparent contest going on to see who could wear the most gold braid. The glitter on the men was only outdone by the gleam of the women's jewels and the clashing colors of their court gowns.

Even without her motoring coat and scarf, Megan felt downright dowdy in her plum-colored velvet traveling suit. But apparently it didn't matter what a princess wore. The peacock-hued lords and ladies all bowed and curtsied as she made her way into the center of the room.

Where was the infamous Gray Piotr?

Over the bobbing heads Megan noticed an out-of-place group. It looked as if a shadow had been cast over part of the colorful mob. Instead of gorgeous uniforms, the men in the group wore darker colors. Their faces had a harder edge than those of the surrounding nobles—and the swords they wore didn't look like decorations. They seemed to bow to her grudgingly, and one figure in their midst didn't bow at all. He was in uniform, but his jacket and trousers were in shades of gray instead of the garish ensembles worn by most of the men. Light glinted off a monocle in his right eye as he gave her a long, thoughtful look. By now, Megan was close enough to recognize Alan Slaney. But like so many people in this room, he was transformed, and it wasn't just the uniform. His brilliantined hair was parted in the middle, and besides the monocle, he boasted a magnificent handlebar mustache that even now he twirled between his thumb and forefinger.

A villain's mustache, Megan thought. Which was only appropriate, since Alan had cast himself as the villain of the piece—Gray Piotr!

Alan moved from the spot where he'd been standing—right beside the throne, Megan suddenly realized. He advanced through the crowd until he'd almost reached Megan, then gave her a courtly bow.

"Glad to see me home, cousin?" Megan asked coolly.

Alan gave her another bow, clearly hiding a delighted grin. He placed a kiss about an inch above her extended hand. "Let us rather say that I'm relieved. Traveling in foreign lands is always an adventure—not to mention the risks of riding the royal railroad."

"Yes, I've heard my share of odd tales," Meg replied.

His eyes were ironic as his gaze met hers. "I only regret the reason that brings you back from your studies in Wurttemburg. Let us hope for a result that will spare you the rigors of rulership."

A low murmur broke from the onlookers at Gray Piotr's words. Megan pitched her voice to carry over it as she replied. "I am not eager to seize up the crown—but if the time comes, I can only hope to fulfill my royal duties as well as Gregor the king!"

Megan smiled at Alan as the nobles all around them broke into applause. His bow said that she'd won this round—but there was more fighting yet to come.

Court etiquette demanded that she graciously nod and accept greetings from the local aristocrats, so she stood on the dais with the prime minister at one elbow and Gray Piotr at the other. Von Esbach cleverly arranged things so that the bigwigs were first introduced to Megan's traveling companions. That way she had a chance to catch their names. Between those exchanges and the briefing she'd received, she got through the reception line without any obvious problems.

"You must be fatigued after all this unfamiliar effort," Alan Slaney purred as the last noble couple moved away. "Surely you would prefer to go to your own apartments and rest?"

"Only after my friends have been seen to," Megan said firmly. She wasn't about to demonstrate that her unfamiliarity with her new role began with the floor plan of the palace. She turned to von Esbach. "I trust suitable arrangements have been made?"

"I shall show you immediately, my princess," the prime minister replied.

"Then I'll leave you to your ... domestic affairs," Gray Piotr said. One more bow, and he moved to join his hard-looking henchmen.

"Off to plot more mischief, no doubt," von Esbach muttered, watching them go.

"We'll be better able to counter it if we all get some rest," Megan replied in a low voice. "Lead on."

The prime minister led Megan and her friends through yet another set of corridors. "I took the liberty of lodging these gentlemen in the Princess's Tower," von Esbach said. In a lower voice, he added, "Anyone attempting to reach the royal apartments will have to come through here."

Leif nodded. "So then they'll have to get through us."

Open doors showed several pleasant-looking bedrooms. "I also took the liberty of having your luggage brought up," von Esbach said.

"And I'd say that arriving in our rooms makes a perfect place to break the action for this session," Megan added in a softer voice. "We'll meet in my virtual workspace for a quick postmortem. What do you say?"

The boys nodded and headed for their rooms. Megan turned to the prime minister. "Perhaps you would accompany me to my own apartments?"

As soon as Leif was through the door, he gave a silent command to cut out of the Latvinia sim. Rather than awakening in his computer-link couch, however, he blinked and found himself in the new address he'd given his computer—Megan O'Malley's personal Net space.

No accounting for taste, Leif thought as he looked around. Maybe it was a reaction to living in a crowded house with a good-sized family, but Megan's workspace was huge—an amphitheater large enough to accommodate a football game and a good twenty thousand fans.

The setup didn't just give her space—it was *out* in space. Megan's stone amphitheater was set on the surface of Rhea, one of Saturn's numerous satellites. When Leif looked up, the ringed planet loomed overhead, like a grossly swollen, orange-striped moon.

Leif turned his attention from the sky show as David synched in. The other boy simply shook his head. "Well, being a foreign prince certainly beats playing a train porter. But when I chopped that guy's hand off—"

"Real swords—and real consequences," Leif said. "I sure hope that robber was a nonrole-playing character."

David turned appalled eyes towards him. "Don't even *start* going there!" he begged. "I have to believe I was just slicing electrons."

"Hey, if you're not sure of the safety interfaces . . .," Leif teased.

P.J. popped into existence beside him. "Boy, we sure dusted those bad guys!" He blew over the top of his outstretched index finger, as if he were cooling down the muzzle of a gun. "A real action-filled start, before things started getting boring with all the politics."

"Nice review, coming from a politician's son."

P.J. gave Leif a haughty look. "My father is a senator, not a politician."

Leif rolled his eyes. "Yeah. Right."

Before he could say anything more, Megan appeared. She was positively fizzing with joy. "What a great sim!"

"Of course, you're not saying that because you got one of the starring roles," Leif said.

"Just because somebody whacked you before you could show off your prize toadsticker doesn't mean you have to dump all over everybody else's good time," Megan replied tartly. "The question now is—when can we all go back in?"

Everybody's eyes got a slight faraway look as they checked with calendar programs back in their computers. "I've got a lunch tomorrow that will run pretty long," Leif said. "It's a family thing—friends of Dad's from Europe. Maybe in the evening—"

Megan shook her head. "Fencing class."

Leif's lips quirked downward, although he managed to keep the scowl from his face. Megan had played heroes and villains with Alan Slaney in sim today, and she'd be working with him in a real-world class tomorrow. . . .

I'd probably like the guy in other circumstances, Leif thought. *He's clever, creative, and has a sense of humor in creating sims.*

Too bad, then, that the existing circumstances involved Megan O'Malley.

I've got no right to be jealous, Leif told himself.

So why was the situation driving him crazy?

5

Leif walked into his room and was just about ready to cut his link when he heard a familiar sound—the clash of steel. He ran to the open window, stopping only to grab his own sheathed sword. His room had a good vantage of the inner courtyard of the palace, much of which was cultivated as a garden.

Two stories below, on a graveled path, two young officers were dueling—at least, they were trying to. The pair looked like clowns, staggering around with no trace of footwork or any idea of the proper distance from which to launch an attack, swinging their heavy cavalry sabers as if they were trying to chop wood.

Looking down, Leif didn't know whether to laugh or be horrified. Latvinia had only been open for bare hours, and these two idiots had to fool with swordplay in the worst way.

And it *was* the worst way, Leif realized as he continued to watch. The two continued to hack and swat at each other with no rhyme or reason. Somewhere in the Latvinia program, there had to be some basic knowledge of swordsmanship stored for the role-players to tap into. But there was a big difference between knowledge whispered in the back of the brain and knowledge in the muscle and nerve tissue.

These guys could barely handle the weight of the heavy military sabers. Their attempted slashes wobbled in midair. One guy was huffing and puffing, looking as if his arm was going to fall off. The amateur duelists would attack at the same time, their blades clanging together, then rebounding. Or they'd manage to miss, which really scared them as razor-sharp blades whipped far to close to various pieces of their anatomy. Then both of them would fall back, or clumsily lock their blades together, they way they'd seen it done in old flatfilms or historical holodramas.

Leif turned away, unable to watch any more of this travesty.

I hope those guys down there aren't products of the fencing school Megan is attending, he thought. Otherwise, the place should be shut down for taking money under false pretenses.

Shaking his head, he gave an unspoken command to his computer. An eye-blink later, he found himself back home on his computer-link couch. He swung around so his feet touched the floor, got up, and stretched. No matter how much the machinery in the couch tried to keep his muscles toned—and Leif's couch was a pretty expensive one—it still felt better to move around after a long session in veeyar.

A glance at his watch made Leif frown. He'd spent more time in Latvinia than he'd realized.

Apparently, time flies even when I'm having a not-so-good time, he thought. A quick pat to his midsection didn't start any growls of hunger. But Leif padded through the apartment on stocking feet anyway, heading for the kitchen.

Mom and Dad were out showing their European friends the glories of the real New York City, as opposed to the virtual version anybody could visit by synching into the Net. He had more than enough time to take a shower and join them for dinner. Besides, Leif *liked* a cup of coffee after spending any length of time on the Net. It brought the real-life edge back to his brain.

He was sitting on a kitchen stool, watching the coffeemaker brew a cup to his precise specifications, when a sound like chiming silver bells filled the house. Leif took one last, longing look at the coffee still dripping down into the cup, then headed over to the terminal set in the kitchen wall to answer the call. He had to answer. It might be his folks, calling with a change of plan.

Hey, it could even be Megan, calling to talk some more about their afternoon's adventure. She'd probably prefer to talk to Alan Slaney, but he was probably still in the sim, plotting away as Gray Piotr.

Leif activated the phone connection, but the face he saw in the hologram image was neither Megan's nor either of his parents.

The model-perfect facial features, dramatically framed by hair as black as a raven's wing, spoke subtly of expert—and expensive—plastic surgery. After a moment of silence those lovely features arranged themselves into a frown that was more like a sneer. "The polite thing to do when someone calls is to say hello, Leif."

"Hello, Roberta," Leif replied cautiously. "Please forgive me. I was . . . surprised."

As far as Leif was concerned, that was putting it mildly. He liked girls, and enjoyed going out with them—a lot of them. He had a reputation to uphold as playboy-in-training—at least, his friends thought so—and so his social activities were almost mandatory. But problems came along with having an active social life. Or, as his father called it, a volcanic one.

Some girls got possessive. They seemed to see more in a friendship/flirtation than was actually there. A few got scared at life in the fast lane—especially if their parents got involved. Other girls just got nasty, treating Leif like the flavor of the week. No matter what the attitude, more than a few of Leif's relationships had ended in explosive breakups.

But Roberta Hendry was in a class by herself. About a year ago, Leif had enjoyed a pretty wild summer with her, running through the Washington social scene with a bunch of diplomatic brats. Roberta's family was old-money rich—what they called FFV, or "First Family of Virginia." The Hendrys had hung on to their wealth since Virginia was a royal colony of Britain. Investments of some of that wealth made two generations ago in early tech stocks had enlarged the family's fortunes from lavish to obscene. They had more than enough money lying about these days to enjoy Society with a capital *S*.

The only two things the Hendrys hated were publicity, which Roberta's escapades sometimes brought on, and politics, which the Hendrys considered vulgar.

Perhaps that's why Roberta had gone political. Maybe it was some bizarre form of late adolescent rebellion.

Journalists and Net newscasters called her "the radical debutante." By the time they'd broken up, Leif thought she'd just gone plain wacko.

Roberta had taken up a bunch of weird *-isms* that frankly contradicted each other—except that they were all revolutionary in tone.

Leif's interest had quickly sunk to impatience when she started ranting to him about changing the whole social order. Somehow, the rhetoric seemed a bit much when he had to listen to a child of privilege attack his self-made father as a bloodsucking parasite.

Magnus Anderson had worked hard to build the fortune Leif enjoyed. A lot of fine people had gotten jobs from his father's company and good paychecks along the way to that fortune. Leif knew about his father's efforts—at times, he'd even helped with them. So being bad-mouthed by a rich girl whose family counted inherited money for a living got to be a little too much.

Leif and Roberta had argued the politics of privilege, their fights getting louder and louder until the rest of their good-time crowd began to avoid them. But the corker had come after a night they'd spent dancing—Roberta had told a valet-parking attendant that it was his class duty to sabotage all the rich folks' cars in his care. When Leif pointed out that would include her own luxury Dodge SUV, Roberta had used the powerful car to try and run him down.

After that, Leif had returned to New York and succeeded in not talking to Roberta Hendry—until this very surprising call.

"I had an agent checking on the comings and goings from Alan Slaney's childish amusement park," Roberta informed him loftily.

Leif wasn't impressed. If her searchbot had wasted

enough time for him nearly to finish making a cup of coffee before getting to Roberta, the agent wasn't all that great.

Reminded of his coffee, Leif picked up the cup, adding a little sugar. Too bad he couldn't sweeten the beautiful girl floating in front of him. "You know Alan Slaney?" he asked. "I would think that historical simulations in general—and AHSO in particular—would be pretty far down the list of your interests."

"On the contrary," Roberta told him. "The turn-of-the-century era was the breeding ground for some of the great political movements of the twentieth century." She took a deep breath, as if she were tasting something. "Socialism, communism, fascism . . . anarchism. They all came to a great flowering twenty years on either side of 1900. I have a deep and valid interest in the turn of the century."

Her lips curled in that all-too-familiar sneer. "Unlike so many who claim an 'interest' in order to play dress-up!"

Leif blinked. "You're actually taking part in the Latvinia beta-test?"

Roberta nodded. "I was just as surprised to find your name listed among the participants." She gave him a sidelong look. "Actually I was more surprised when your name turned up in the early reports on the sim. My agent sorts items of political importance for me—even the silly reactionary politics in this charade. Imagine my astonishment when I discovered that you had prevented an attempt to kidnap Princess Gwenda! And you're staying in the palace!"

Leif rolled his eyes. "And what exactly do you want out of it?"

Roberta leaned forward, intent on her plans—and

completely oblivious to Leif's skeptical reaction. "I'll be entering Latvinia as Viola da Gamba, an adventurous female reporter." Her lips twisted again. "It was the least demeaning role I could find in the simulation. I'm sure Slaney planned it that way, to keep me from upsetting his reactionary applecart. As a commoner, I would normally find it almost impossible to speak to the princess, even though I represent the press."

"Normally," Leif repeated.

"But now I have a friend at court—literally," Roberta said with a self-satisfied nod.

Ignoring her rather elastic definition of "friend"— someone who chases you down the street in a car with probable intent to kill wasn't anywhere on Leif's definition of *friendship*—Leif asked, "Isn't there someone else in the SIG you can . . . uh . . . get help from?"

If Roberta had been scornful before, she got three times worse now. "Those . . . idiots! They have no notion of the importance of the era. For the girls, it's a chance to try on so-called 'romantic' fashions. And the boys all leap into uniforms, playing soldier. It's the same heedless imperialism that got millions killed in 1914—"

"I'll take that as a simple 'no,' then," Leif said.

Roberta's voice became suspiciously sugary. "But you, Leif . . . even though we weren't on the same political plane, you always liked to make things happen. I'd say it's safe to assume that Slaney doesn't know we have a history. Imagine the look on his face when you usher me in for an interview with the princess!"

Oh, it wouldn't be an interview, Leif knew. Viola da Gamba would start lecturing "Princess Gwenda" on everything she saw wrong with Latvinian society. Megan would be ready to kill him by the time it was over.

Even so, Leif couldn't quite keep the grin off his lips. Anything that might annoy the great Alan Slaney was all right with him. . . .

The next day at the fencing salle, Alan had to crack down and make people work—everyone was talking about Latvinia and their adventures there.

Megan found herself standing in front of a mirror, working off her distraction by practicing moulinets—the deadly diagonal cuts Alan had used to harass her during their last practice. The idea was to make the cut as efficiently and quickly as possible—with perfect form. Twist the wrist, slash up with the sword from left to right. Then take the *en garde* stance with the blade defending the right, and slash up from there—

"You do not do it correctly," the practice partner, Sergei Chernevsky, suddenly said.

"What's wrong?" Megan asked. Sergei had been studying at the salle longer than she had. If he could give her the benefit of his experience . . .

"You move the blade like a modern fencer—with the flat. Listen." His blade flashed up, making an audible *whiff*ing noise.

"Classical moulinet means leading with the edge. You can hear the difference." His sword leaped up again, but this time there was a whistle as the blade's edge cut the air.

"I see," Megan said. "Actually, I hear." They grinned at each other, then resumed their positions. Up and around—*slice!* Down and around—*slice!*

Soon Megan's blade began to whistle instead of whisper as she got the trick of it. She also began to get a sweaty face and an aching arm. "I really, really hope this is an important move," she puffed.

Sergei's breathing was a bit labored, too. "I read about some old-time fencing masters, they would expect you to do thirty minutes' worth—moulinet with lunge."

"Great." Megan laughed. "Burn out your legs *and* your arm."

They resumed their practice. "By the way," Megan added as her sword whistled through the air, "I was very impressed by your uniform in the sim."

"It is the costume of the old Hungarian Hussars," Sergei replied. "Embroidered frogging across the chest, and the fur-trimmed jacket—the pelisse—worn over one shoulder."

He smiled as he swung his sword around. "The saber, you know, came from Hungary. The cavalry there adopted it from the Turkish scimitar." Sergei actually blushed. "Excuse the lecture. Back home, I went to a military school. Every cadet had to learn the motherland's glorious military history. I was always fascinated by swords and cavalry. My dream was to be a Hussar."

He brought his blade around with a flourish, slicing his moulinets back and forth, creating a sideways figure eight in steel.

"Even more impressive," Megan said. "Except that it looks like the sign for infinity."

"Let us hope Alan does not keep us that long on the exercise," Sergei said. "It is supposed to make the fingers more flexible, the wrist more limber."

"If my wrist gets any more limber, my hand will fall off." Megan glanced in the mirror, searching for their instructor in the reflection. "Where did Alan go?"

Sergei took a break, shrugging. "Disappeared, just like the kidnappers in the sim. We followed their trail right onto the slopes of the great mountain—Grauheim. But we couldn't find another trace."

Transferring her saber to her left hand, Megan shook out her right, trying to get the lactic acid out of her burning muscles. Then, gritting her teeth, she resumed the practice.

So, the guys who got the real Princess Gwenda disappeared on the slopes of Grauheim, the wildest mountain in Latvinia. Not surprising.

Especially not surprising, if Gray Piotr, Master of Grauheim, was behind the plot to steal the throne. What was Alan Slaney up to behind that monocle and mustache?

"You've lost your whistle again." Sergei's voice intruded on her thoughts.

Megan blinked, glaring at her sword as the flat whiffled through the air instead of the edge slicing. She resumed the guard position for the left side of her body, concentrating on every move.

Can't do this right if you don't think of what you're doing, she scolded herself. *Fencing now. Latvinia later.*

She shook her head as her blade whistled through the air.

Damn, but Alan had created a seductive little world!

6

For about the fifteenth time since he'd synched into Latvinia, Leif tried to readjust the uniform he wore. It wasn't that the crimson-and-gold jacket and light gray trousers didn't fit him. It was more that the perfectly tailored uniform fit a little too well. The cavalry trousers tucked into knee-high boots felt more like ski pants—or possibly like a pair of tights. His memory of that exposed feeling, a natural result of taking lessons at his mother's ballet school, was one of the few unpleasant ones he'd taken from his stint as a boy dancer. The pants he had now were what they'd have called spray-ons way back in the disco era. Skin tight and a bit too blatant. And his Hussar-style jacket only came to his waist. In this 1890s style, he felt as though everyone was checking out parts of him that guys didn't generally show off in public in the year 2025.

But it was the wish of the princess that he become an honorary member of the Royal Guard, complete with fancy uniform and a sword at his side. Leif suspected that Megan took a secret glee in seeing him prancing around like this. P.J. had adopted the uniform, too, with the addition of his cowboy hat. David—or rather, Men-elik—had flatly refused to wear the rig, preferring his royal robes.

Unfortunately, Leif didn't have any native dress to use as an excuse to get out of this costume. He wouldn't see Megan until the royal court late in the afternoon, so he'd decided to spend his free time exploring the palace and trying to get used to his new clothes.

And there had been one other piece of business. A note had come from Viola da Gamba, just arrived in Herzen, asking her old friend Hengist to help her get an interview with Princess Gwenda. As he'd promised the night before, Leif had passed along the request to the Graf von Esbach and the royal appointments secretary. They had assured Leif that his friend would be received at court that very day.

The good effect of the day's wanderings was that Leif had a much better idea of the geography inside the royal palace. On the bad side of the ledger were the several duels Leif had witnessed. The would-be swordsmen had ranged from merely incompetent to dangerously inept. One duelist had lost control of his saber during a wild slash and sliced into his own leg.

Leif had offered a little first aid with an improvised tourniquet—and began to appreciate why the code du-ello required that a physician be on hand. Unfortunately, these amateurs hadn't taken that elementary precaution. Leif had managed to keep the failed swordsman "alive" until medical help had arrived. But he suspected this guy would spend most of the beta-testing period of this sim waiting for his wound to heal.

Strolling along, hand on the hilt of his own blade, Leif shook his head. It was just as well that Alan Slaney hadn't included an actual Ostwald in his sim. If it came to out-and-out war between the two vest-pocket states, there wouldn't be enough officers to lead that Latvinian army—too many of the players would have put themselves on the injured list with stupid sword tricks.

At last the time came for royal audiences. Leif marched to the entrance of the throne room, where he found P.J. and David already waiting.

P.J. gave him a grin as big as Texas. "You look like the doorman for a very expensive, but slightly kinky, hotel," he told Leif.

"Can it, cowboy," Leif replied. "Keep in mind you're wearing the same uniform. Have either of you caught up with Meg—the princess—today?"

"I saw her briefly, when I regretfully declined to wear that insane costume," David said. "She was halfway through a royal makeover—I can hardly wait to see the final results."

When Megan arrived, accompanied by the Graf von Esbach, Colonel Vojak, and a company of guards, Leif could see what David meant. Megan's usual cloud of dark curls had been coiled carefully around her head, and a diadem of gold and jewels sat above her forehead. The style suited her all too well. She was a knockout. She wore a magnificent low-cut off-white court gown and a stern expression on her features—the result of royal cares . . . or maybe annoyance at the enforced changes in her look. Megan had never been a silk-and-ruffles kind of girl.

The bewigged flunkies threw open the throne room

doors, and the court sorted itself out. A few changes had been made, including the addition of a simple seat on the step below the royal throne. That was where Megan sat. Von Esbach, Vojak, David, Leif, and P.J. took positions to the right of the throne. Gray Piotr and a knot of his tough guys stood off to the left.

Another flunky who looked like a refugee from Colonial Williamsburg stood by the door, brandishing a large parchment scroll. He raised it and began speaking in German, announcing people as they came to be presented at court.

After several ambassadors had bowed to the princess, the name of Viola da Gamba was announced. Roberta Hendry swept into the throne room with all the poise that life as a jet-set debutante had given her. She wore a plum-colored velvet riding suit with a matching hat set at a perky angle—and a smile of triumph as she looked at Alan Slaney. The Master of Grauheim—not to mention the creator of Latvinia—was not pleased to see her in the royal presence.

Roberta stepped to the dais where Megan sat. "Your Majesty, it is a pleasure to visit Latvinia, and a privilege to be in your presence." She sank into a graceful curtsy, but her tone was almost challenging as she went on. "I hope to discuss the true state of the realm with you—"

Then disaster struck as Roberta came out of her curtsy. Although she must have practiced the move a million times in dance classes and at debutante balls, the heel of her boot caught in the hem of her riding habit's skirt. Roberta rose to a ripping sound—and her velvet skirt crumpled gracefully down until it was merely a purple ring around Roberta's ankles.

The color of the young woman's face almost matched the hue of her clothing as she stood in front of the assembled nobility in jacket, ascot, and a pair of shapeless lilac bloomers.

Some gallant soul—one of the diplomats, no doubt trained to meet social disasters—leaped forward with a cape to cover Roberta's humiliation.

Leif couldn't help himself. He burst into laughter, turning to pass a quiet comment to P.J. "It's a shame about those bloomers, really. Roberta's got a pair of legs worth looking at."

He was laughing again when a heavy hand landed on his shoulder. "Sir," a harsh voice said in French, "must you add to this young lady's embarrassment?"

Leif turned to confront a guy who might as well have had the title "Villain's Henchman" embroidered on his chest. The Frenchman was shorter than Leif, thick-bodied, with a head like a cannonball. His haircut was more like a shave job, but he boasted luxurious mustachios over his close-cropped beard. He wore a plain gray and green uniform with officer's insignia, and he had a soldier's air of command.

Just one look, and Leif disliked him immediately. "I think it would be hard to go beyond the embarrassment the young lady has brought upon herself," he said coolly, turning away.

Again he found that hand on his shoulder. "It is not appropriate for a gentleman to make such a remark."

Now Leif was getting angry. "Why don't you mind your own business instead of my manners?"

The Frenchman looked up into his eyes. "Because you obviously need instruction."

Leif's hand clenched on the hilt of his sword. "And are you going to give it to me?"

"Right now would be opportune." The Frenchman pulled out the riding gloves tucked into his saber belt and threw one at Leif's feet. "Name your seconds."

For a second Leif stood with his mouth open.

Oh, wonderful, he thought. *I've gotten myself into a duel.* He turned to his friends. David wore his scimitar, but P.J. was weaponless. For him an affair of honor would be settled with an old-fashioned Western fistfight. "I'm afraid my friends are ignorant of the conventions—"

The Frenchman turned to a young Hussar officer. "You—be his second."

The big, gorgeously uniformed young man blinked in shock, then presented his hand to Leif. "Sergei Chernevsky, at your service."

Another officer was drafted to officiate over the meeting, as the code duello demanded. Moments later the duelists and their seconds were heading out a pair of French windows into the long shadows in the palace courtyard.

"The walled garden over there will serve the purpose," said the officer now running the duel. "We'll have no glare of dying sunlight. But we'll need a physician— ah, Herr Doktor Fleischer!" The officer turned to Leif. "Doktor Fleischer is the army surgeon."

Leif nodded. "We've met." This was the medical man who'd been called to stitch together the unfortunate duelist he'd patched up so recently.

Now it might be Leif's turn. . . .

The doctor took in the advancing party and gave an "oh, no, not again!" headshake.

"You have your bag, Doctor? Excellent! Then let us proceed before we lose the light." The military man led the way into the garden.

Numbly Leif slipped out of his coat, handing it to David. Things were moving so fast! While the seconds prepared a space, he began warming up as if this were a fencing bout, jumping up and down, stretching his muscles. He held the blade over his head, bending it. Then he settled into a fencing stance, making quick, flashing moves with his blade, limbering up his wrist and fingers.

"Most athletic," the Frenchman said dryly. He stood perfectly still, executing multiple moulinets with the heavy cavalry saber. To Leif, it looked more as though his opponent were leading a band instead of getting ready for a deadly fight. Well, he looked as if he knew what to do with the sword. And the guy wasn't even breaking into a sweat.

Leif's mouth suddenly felt dry.

At least we'll do better than those other idiots I've seen playing at swords, he promised himself.

The Frenchman ceased his warm-up cuts. "Are you prepared, m'sieur?"

Leif nodded, afraid to trust his voice.

The officiating officer stepped up. "Gentlemen, present your weapons, please." The pre-duel inspection was quickly accomplished. "Step back, please."

Leif went into his usual offensive guard position, free hand held loose at his side, his arm slightly bent to present the blade toward the Frenchman's eyes.

His opponent's free hand was fisted on his hip as he took a very erect, almost prissy pose, his arm almost at a right angle, holding out his sword.

The officiating officer drew his own saber, placing it between the crossed blades of the two antagonists. He raised his arm, separating the blades for a moment. "*Allez!*" he cried. "Forward!"

Leif felt a moment of confidence. The Frenchman's stance could be a textbook illustration of the old-fashioned way of doing things. The placement of the blade left part of the guy's arm exposed! Leif moved to attack, going for a cut at that arm. The Frenchman merely stepped aside, not even bothering to parry. Nor, however, did he riposte.

Well, Leif thought, *he's got a big hunk of metal to move.* He continued to play his athletic game, moving back and forth, feinting with the blade, not initiating any contact with the other man's steel.

The Frenchman stood as if his feet were rooted to the ground. Leif came forward again. This time his opponent's saber moved—and with blurring speed. The back end of the Frenchman's blade beat against Leif's sword, disrupting his move, then the point of the enemy's saber flew at Leif's face. It could have cut him, leaving a disfiguring scar or worse. Leif's opponent was merely demonstrating a possibility.

Leif desperately backpedaled, pulling back his arm and blade, astonished. In two whistling moves the Frenchman had derailed Leif's attack—and presented a much more pointed threat.

How can he be so fast? Leif asked himself. *And with that huge, old-fashioned cavalry saber?*

With a chill he realized that his champion-grade competitive fencer muscles couldn't move this heavy steel that quickly.

Still, he stayed with his weaving movements.

Float like a butterfly, he thought, *and hope for a chance to sting.*

The Frenchman suddenly advanced, swinging another lightning circular cut at Leif—a moulinet. Leif tried to parry, but the other sword was so fast—the tip of cold steel just barely caressed his cheek. It could have been another devastating cut, if the Frenchman had followed through. But this had been merely a test. And Leif had failed.

"You could, perhaps, use schooling in more than manners," the Frenchman told him.

Leif didn't answer, saving his breath for his running game. It had always worked for him before, tiring out the other side.

But this opponent didn't run. He stood easily, his sword flicking back and forth, the point always in Leif's face. Leif tried to parry, to engage the other man's blade. But the point seemed to leap away from his deflecting attempts.

Leif was beginning to sweat. How could his opponent do that? The guy wasn't even extending his arm!

Then the Frenchman was coming forward, his blade flashing in multiple moulinets. Leif was driven back, managing to parry the first two. *False attacks,* he thought. *He's still testing me.*

The third blow, however, was completely unorthodox. Leif nearly staggered, leaping back after the flat of the Frenchman's sword heartily tapped against his thigh.

"Your low line is weak," the Frenchman said, as if he were a fencing master.

Leif almost opened his mouth to yell foul—the conventional saber target is anything from the waist up. But he closed his mouth with a snap as an unwelcome piece of information popped up from the sim programming. In this era the front thigh was indeed a valid target.

He was startled—no one had ever attacked him there with a saber. Leif was also feeling a little afraid. He'd plunged into this against an unknown opponent. And now it seemed he also didn't know the rules.

Well, turnabout is fair play, he thought, leaping in with a looping cut for the Frenchman's extended leg.

Instead, his antagonist's blade tapped against his fore-arm—another potentially devastating stop-cut, if the Frenchman had swung in earnest. "Touché," the bearded man announced, as if they were indeed on a fencing *piste*.

Leif desperately worked for distance, now. He needed the space for a running attack—a *fleche*. He flung himself at the Frenchman, deliberately letting himself go off-balance as he advanced in a giant step. But his target was nowhere near his blade. The Frenchman neither attacked nor defended—he merely stepped aside. Leif stumbled to a stop, to find that his opponent had swung around, giving him a very Gallic shrug. "You missed."

Now Leif lost it, hurling himself forward into another running attack, sword raised for a head cut. *This time,* he thought, *the guy wouldn't move away!*

The Frenchman didn't. He moved forward, *into* Leif's attack, his blade across his body, parallel with the ground. Neither the Frenchman's point nor the sharp-ened edges of his saber threatened Leif. . . . But the metal guard that protected the swordsman's hand was in a direct line with Leif's jaw. There was no way to stop, to turn away. Running full-tilt, Leif rammed into the equivalent of brass knuckles backed by a very muscular arm, shoulder, and body.

"Better than killing you, puppy," the Frenchman said.

Then it was lights out for Leif.

Leif opened his eyes with a wince, finding himself on his computer-link couch in 2025 New York. "Ouch!" he muttered. "Knocked right out of the sim!"

Gingerly he rubbed his temples. His head throbbed a little, but it wasn't as bad as the headache that came with a system crash.

Of course, that didn't factor in the hit his pride had just taken—

Leif didn't have time to fret over that for very long. The communications chime sounded from his computer. Someone was calling. He responded, and Roberta Hendry's furious face appeared in holo projection. "That was a lousy thing you did, Anderson," she accused. "Setting me up like that."

"Setting you up? Me?" Leif said in confusion. "Not bloody likely—unless you think my idea of a big payoff is getting my butt kicked. I had words with one of Gray Piotr's goons"—better not to say what it was about, he decided—"and found myself in the most one-sided duel—or fencing match or whatever you want to call it—of my life."

Roberta calmed down slightly as she considered what Leif had said. "It has to be Slaney, then, who set me up," she finally said viciously. "That worm has always hated my politics—he thinks they're a stain on his little aristocratic fairyland." She gave Leif a sidelong look. "And it would seem that sword-boy has some sort of problem with your fencing reputation. Could it be jealousy?"

Leif shook his head. "Two completely different styles—they don't even intersect. Slaney and his friends are essentially academic—preserving the old forms that aren't used much anymore. I'm into the sport end—you know, competition."

"Maybe that's exactly what he sees you as," Roberta cut in, "Competition. Does he know about your championships?"

Thinking about the enormous database form that he'd filled out, Leif could only shrug. "Yeah, I'm sure it got mentioned somewhere in the character profile. But, still—"

Roberta, however, had heard everything she wanted to hear. She leaned in towards her system pickup. "I've got friends on the national board of AHSO—at least my parents do. We shouldn't let Slaney get away with this. A strong enough protest to the right people would get Latvinia shut down."

Leif couldn't believe what he was hearing. "For what?" he said, pouring cold water on Roberta's idea. "You could have suffered an accident. And I didn't have the brains to check up on the guy who called me out. Neither incident can be pinned to Slaney, and they're hardly mortal offenses even if we could prove he was behind them."

He shrugged, suddenly wondering how Megan would feel if somebody pulled the plug on Latvinia. "Besides, it's just a sim—a fantasy."

On the other side of the connection, Roberta had calmed down a little—not necessarily a good sign. She had gotten over getting mad. Now she was into getting even. When she answered Leif, every word seemed to come out like a drop of venom.

"Maybe that's what Alan Slaney needs to learn," Roberta said. "That his fantasies can have real-life consequences."

7

Megan had gotten as far as the French doors to the court-yard before the Graf von Esbach caught up with her—and gently stopped her.

"Your Majesty," he said softly, "it would be most improper for you of all people to witness that duel."

The background knowledge programmed into the sim backed him up a hundred percent. Duels were supposed to be private affairs—audiences were frowned upon. Female audiences were especially frowned upon, although there were a couple of scandalous historical references. But for a member of a royal house to involve him- or herself in such an irregular affair . . .

In properly old-fashioned terms it just wasn't done.

Megan's initial response was the urge to yell "Frack that!" and go to back up Leif, regardless of the consequences.

But then, she wasn't really Megan O'Malley in this here and now. She was in a sim, playing Marguerite O'Malley, adventurous society girl masquerading as Princess Gwenda. Marguerite would never use language like "Frack that!" And the real princess wouldn't be caught dead at a duel.

Standing beside her, the older man watched the duelists head off for the walled garden. Then he glanced at Megan. "You and the baron . . . is it a matter of the heart?"

Megan shot the old guy a look that could have scorched off his side whiskers. "We're just friends," she snapped. Then, in a lower voice, "If I were the real princess—"

"I would never have dared to ask such a thing," von Esbach finished for her in equally quiet tones. "However, dear lady, I am fighting for the life of my country. So I will risk an impertinent question if it will help discover a weakness to be defended." He nodded toward the garden. "Even as our antagonist seeks out any weaknesses he can exploit."

Megan's hand went to her mouth. "That man who challenged Leif—the baron—"

"One of Gray Piotr's creatures." Von Esbach almost spat out the word. "He's an unknown foreign adventurer, given rank in our army by the Master of Grauheim."

The prime minister bit off any further words as Gray Piotr himself approached. Once again he seemed to be scanning Megan with his monocle. Searching for signs of weakness?

"Your Majesty," Piotr murmured. "You left the court in such haste that many were surprised. Some even thought you were going off to witness the vulgar spectacle outside."

Oh, I'm sure your stooges are even now spreading that particular bit of dirt, Megan grimly thought.

She looked hard at the face, so like the Alan Slaney she admired . . . and yet so different.

"You can tell the court that I shall return—"

When I'm damn well good and ready, a rebellious voice piped up from the back of Megan's head.

"Presently," she finished aloud, deciding a more diplomatic tone was appropriate.

Then she ruined the effect by gasping as the gate of the walled garden swung open. Four men were carrying another. And even at that distance, she could make out the red hair on the lolling head.

"Is he—?" She couldn't force the words out.

Gray Piotr's mask of aristocratic irony cracked. He muttered some sort of command, and everything around them—the palace corridor, the courtyard outside—went gray. Beside them, Graf von Esbach stood frozen like a store mannequin or some hyper-realistic statue.

"Don't worry," Alan said—and it *was* Alan speaking, not Gray Piotr. "I'm just freezing the sim for a moment. It's hard to play a character and get all the information you want."

His face got a distant look, as if he were listening to a faraway voice. "You're friend's fine. No blood shed— he just got knocked unconscious. In fact, that's a simulacrum they're carrying. The real Leif synched out."

His smile of relief turned less pleasant. "So did Roberta Hendry, after her curtsy showed off more than she intended. The Viola da Gamba leaving the court is just a simulacrum, too."

He waved an arm at the scene. "I thought you'd like to know that everything's okay. This is just cleaning up the set."

Alan readjusted his monocle, and Graf von Esbach and everyone else came back to life. But a thoughtful frown remained on Megan's face all the way back to the throne room.

Megan had a different reason to frown during the next night's fencing practice. She was working with Sergei again, against the antagonist in the mirror—her reflection. They were practicing footwork and unexpected moves, one calling out orders as they both moved. "Advance! Retreat! Lunge!" Sergei called out.

Attacks with the point of the saber were valid in historical fencing, but hard to pull off successfully. By the time an attacker closed the distance, an alert defender could usually parry. A point attack was a trick that had to be pulled sparingly, at the right time . . . and at the right speed. Megan hadn't expected Sergei's command, and bobbled as she thrust.

Sighing, she tried to do better with her next movements. "Retreat! Pass to the rear!" This was another tricky move. The standard fencing retreat was the reverse of the advance—pushing off on the forward foot, gliding the rear foot back about a foot and a half, then matching the movement with the forward foot to retain the *en garde* position. The movement was harder than it looked, because it had to be done smoothly, without making her weapon jump around. The *passata* was even stranger, a crablike quickstep executed at ninety degrees to the way she was used to walking. Megan's sword point wobbled as she tried to move and guard herself at the same time.

And they weren't even trying to do it quickly yet!

Sergei let her retreat a few more times, then began directing a new advance on the mirror. "By the way," he said as they took a brief rest, "I was approached to betray you yesterday."

Megan shot a look at Sergei, then her eyes sought the mirror, looking for their instructor. "Was it Alan—Gray Piotr?"

With a laugh, Sergei shook his head. "It is a very different plot, I fear—with a very different motive. There are several AHSO members, prominent in the SIG, who are annoyed at the part you have been given."

For a second, Megan didn't even know how to answer. "It's a sim, for frack's sake! A beta-test? Maybe they should get a life."

"Apparently the life they have chosen is historical simulation," Sergei replied. "From the note I received, they seem very jealous that an outsider received such a major role. They appealed to my sense of fairness to help in rectifying this mistake."

"Do you know these people?" Megan asked.

Sergei shrugged. "I am not an AHSO member myself. But they seem willing enough to allow me to play the lowly bodyguard." He drew himself up, his sword at the ready. "Do they think a Hussar would fail to defend his princess?"

Megan didn't know whether to laugh or be touched. "I guess they're not thinking much at all," she finally said. "I mean, it's a game."

Her frown returned as she remembered another game she'd been involved with. One of the players had really gone off the deep end, attacking his role-playing rivals in real life.

"Perhaps I should have played along, found out who was behind the note." Sergei sounded a little embarrassed.

"What did you do?"

The Russian boy's face grew a little pink. "I tore the note up and threw it in the messenger's face."

Megan couldn't hide her smile. "Very much in character."

"You're a *Korpsbruder*—er, sister. I mean, we're fellow fencers together."

"And I guess we should get back to fencing," she said, before he began to babble. "My turn to give the commands, I think. Retreat! Retreat! Retreat! Pass forward!"

At least now the tempo and body movements were things she could control. . . .

"I hope you know what you're doing," David said tightly on his next visit to Latvinia. Against his better judgment, Leif and P.J. had persuaded him to get up on a horse. Except for a couple of fun-fair pony rides as a little kid, he'd never been in the saddle. It wasn't something kids from the streets of urban Washington did much, even in veeyar.

"Just follow your instincts," P.J. told him, reining in the high-stepping stallion he'd chosen. Leif's mount was a bit less spirited, but he seemed comfortable enough in the saddle. Riding was probably another of those elite sports he'd been trained in.

David tried to grip tighter with his legs. The ground seemed an awfully long way down as they clopped along. "My instincts tell me to get off and hail an autocab," he muttered unhappily.

"P.J. picked a gentle horse, we won't go far, and you won't have to do anything extreme," Leif promised. "It's just to get you used to the saddle, in case this adventure takes us someplace the car can't go."

"Doesn't the programming give you any help?" P.J. asked.

"There's not even as much support as I got on swords-manship," David said, trying to listen for any help routines. "And you might remember, that wasn't all that useful, either."

"You came through the first sword fight just fine." P.J. tried to sound encouraging.

"Sure, by accident, and except for wanting to lose my lunch," David pointed out.

"Well, if we're lucky, Slaney won't have programmed in saddle sores," Leif said. "How about once more around the stable yard? That way if you fall, you'll only land in mud."

"Great," David muttered as he led his horse into a turn. "Wonderful."

As the boys swung round, they caught an unexpected dash of color entering the stable yard. It was Roberta Hendry—Viola da Gamba—this time in a bright red riding habit.

The area near the gate was full of people. A large group of country types—peasants—were talking with the stable hands while hitching pairs of draft mules to crude two-wheeled wagons loaded with hay.

Roberta stepped decisively to an empty wagon and stepped up on the tongue of a wagon where the mules were about to be yoked, which rested down on the muddy ground. "Comrades!" she called out. "I would call you my friends, but I won't—not until I've proven my friendship. I call you comrades, because that is what we should be—comrades in a struggle against an unjust and arbitrary social system! A system which demands that you lie quietly while others stand upon your backs and press your faces into the mud!"

"Well, she picked a good place to talk about that,"

P.J. said, looking at the brownish, mushy ground around them.

"Roberta always thought the peasants should be revolting." Leif shook his head. "Ask me, they already are! Have you taken a good whiff? Equal parts garlic breath and B.O."

"That was probably an old joke even in this era," David told him.

Roberta, meanwhile, was really getting into her speech. "The rich, the powerful, they'll say you can improve yourselves—work hard, and you'll become men of property.

"That, of course, is a lie. Not merely because they'll only let you have whatever property they don't want, but because *all* property is theft!"

She clambered onto one of the wagon's wheels so she could look down at her audience. "If you seek the comfort of religion—well, that comfort is only found in the next world, not in this one. 'The poor are always with us,' the churchmen say. And so it will be—so long as the rich continue to steal the wealth that belongs to all of us!"

Her eyes raked their way across the growing crowd of upturned faces. "And what of the powerful? What of those like your dear princess, who claims to be *concerned* for you all?" Roberta made the word sound like some sort of curse. "Oh, she and those like her will do all they can to help you—except get off your backs! What are the lives of a few—if the world is to be changed?"

"Great crib job," Leif said. "I think I detect quotes from everywhere—early socialists, anarchists, and that last one came from Mussolini, if I remember."

"What I don't understand is why she's wasting her

time," David muttered. "Those folks all have to be nonrole-playing characters. Who'd sign up to come here and just shovel horse dooky?"

P.J. stared at the crowd, which was beginning to stir. "Maybe she knows something we don't about the programming here—or maybe she has a few friends in the crowd."

The stable hands and peasants did seem to be responding to Roberta's fire-eating speech.

"Now is the time to rise!" Roberta's voice was a clarion call. "Your so-called betters pretend to despise you, but in truth, that's really fear. They try to distract you with a pretty piece of cloth—a flag. They throw a few pennies at you, and expect you to be content. They build cannon to threaten you. But what good will those cannon be, if the cannoneers are on our side? Rise up, I say, rise! You have nothing to lose but your chains!"

Carried along by her own oratory, she leaped up onto the two-wheeled cart itself. The sudden shift of weight made the wagon abruptly tip. Roberta tumbled from her perch, her fall broken by a giant pile of mud behind the cart.

All three boys waved their hands before their faces in a fruitless attempt to ward off the sudden stink rushing toward them. That wasn't mud at all. Roberta had just discovered the location of the stable's muckheap the hard way.

"Whoof!" David managed, his eyes watering. "It seems they feed the horses well in these parts."

Roberta's former audience simply fell apart, roaring with laughter. The sudden movement and noise spooked David's mount, which broke into a nervous trot, moving through a lane appearing in the dispersing crowd.

"Whoa, horse," David said nervously, sawing on the

reins in an effort to slow his mount down. The horse paid no attention to his efforts, beginning to buck a little as it came closer to the mound of horse flop from which a bemired Roberta was emerging.

Apparently, her appearance was the last straw for David's mount. It began making serious efforts to get its rider off its back.

David gave up all pretense of being in charge of things. "HELLLLLP!" he yelled.

Which would make for a softer landing? he wondered as he crouched low in the saddle, clinging as best he could. *Should I aim for the mud, or for Mount Crapola over there?*

He was barely aware of P.J. coming up from the side, swinging down from the saddle. The young Texan approached David's mount, who was showing a lot of white around the eyes. "Hey, big feller," P.J. said in a soft voice. "Simmer down, simmer down."

The horse shied, tossing its head, but before it could rear, P.J. got hold of the reins. "Nobody's gonna hurt you."

"I wouldn't mind getting off if that would make him happy," David said in a strangled voice.

"Shhhhh," P.J. said.

David wasn't sure if that comment was aimed at him or the horse P.J. was trying to gentle. At least the blasted animal wasn't trying to fling him off anymore.

P.J. finally indicated to David that it was safe to dismount. Luckily, he'd maneuvered them all into an area where the brown muck covering the ground really was mud, and not something worse.

"We'll have to try this again—real soon," David said, rubbing his aching muscles as P.J. began to lead both his own horse and David's former mount away. "I just can't remember when I've had this much fun."

Leif Anderson sat in his saddle, watching Roberta Hendry storm off, heedlessly squelching through mud puddles. Knowing Roberta, she'd probably synched out as soon as she realized what she'd landed in. If her simulacrum was that angry, how furious was the real-life original?

Looks like Latvinia is downright hostile to good old Roberta, Leif thought as the simulacrum vanished through the stable gates. *Is she going to keep fighting . . . or will she just make good on her threats to get this place shut down?*

Megan did her best to hide a yawn, and then fought the
impulse to reach up and scratch her head vigorously.
This *has* to be a sim, she told herself. In real life her
hair would have escaped even these tight braids surrounding the gold and diamond diadem at her brow.

She supposed she should enjoy the unfamiliar experience of having an orderly hairstyle. Instead, she felt as
though the braids were squashing her brain. That didn't
improve her mood—nor did sitting through a deadly
boring afternoon in the throne room. Megan made a
mental note to avoid these lesser courts as much as possible and let her simulacrum handle them. She probably
should have been saving her energy for the royal ball
this evening.

Apparently, the townsfolk of Herzen had a long and
glorious tradition of bringing their disputes to be settled

by their monarch instead of going to the local magistrates. Megan found herself being asked to act like Solomon in cases she barely knew anything about. She did her best to listen carefully, to resolve things fairly—and to make things hot for anyone who looked to be abusing their royal privileges.

I hope I'm getting the hang of this, Megan thought.

Then the two large families came before the throne, each clan looking daggers at the other. The people bringing the suit were Herzen townspeople. As far as Megan could make out from their complaints in German, the problem seemed to revolve around a missing bridegroom and a failure to pay thirteen goats. The other family group was more rural—peasants painfully dressed in their Sunday best.

When it was the turn of these folks to put their case, they broke into torrents of what could only be native Latvinian. Megan couldn't say if this was some sort of Serbo-Croatian dialect or plain gibberish. It was odd that she was having trouble with translation—normally the Net provided instantaneous translation of every language and dialect imaginable.

A smug voice came from the crowd of courtiers. "Surely the princess will understand the old speech of the country folk?"

Yeah, the princess would understand it—but not her American stand-in, Megan thought sourly, *at least not without some help I'm not getting right now. Looks like word of my Great Imposture is going to leak out.*

Megan held up her hand. The spokesman for the peasants, an older man with an enormous mustache, immediately stopped talking. "I beg the great one's pardon," he said more slowly. "Our feelings run before the horses."

Megan managed not to gawk when she realized that the man was still talking in Latvinian—and now she was understanding him perfectly! She wondered what had gone wrong to block the translation, and what was now going suddenly right?

Another of those pseudo-memories implanted by the simulation program whispered through her brain—something about being taught the language as a child by a distant relative of her mother's.

That didn't matter—so long as she could answer the peasant spokesman in his own dialect. "You are pardoned, as long as your words do not fly like the birds," she said. "Continue, Oldfather—only slowly."

The old peasant had quite a story to tell. It seemed the city slickers were making a good thing out of the betrothal visits. They'd enter into contracts with peasants in the surrounding districts, specifying a wedding within a certain amount of time or a bride-price in livestock. Then, one of the bride-to-be's uncles—a recruiting sergeant for the army—made sure the prospective bridegrooms were conscripted and taken off before the weddings could take place.

As the old man continued, a rather military-looking member of the city family tried to vanish among the ranks of his relatives.

Grim-faced, Megan had him hauled forth and put him to some searching questions—both in German and Latvinian.

The poor sergeant was in a sweat. "Majesty, we would never have troubled you, except—"

One of the quicker-minded female members of the family kicked him in the ankle.

"We would never have brought this case, except those

dirt-eaters insulted Your Majesty," the leader of the city clan quickly said.

Megan continued her interrogation, finally digging out the information that the family ran a thriving butcher shop in the town, and was amassing money to expand the business. By the time she was finished, they'd still be in business, but in a much less prosperous fashion.

Just like those real-life courtroom entertainment holos, she thought, giving her judgment. Megan glanced again at the quivering sergeant, wondering who had put the city slickers up to bringing this case before her. Was it a trick by Gray Piotr?

She turned to where Alan Slaney stood, off to the side of the throne. His expression was a mixture of amusement and annoyance as he watched the case progress to judgement. Aware of her eyes on him, he looked up. "Did they think I couldn't plan ahead a little better than that?"

Megan hid a smile. So, the courtroom drama was an attempt to embarrass her by jealous AHSO members.

Her smile slipped a little. Unless Alan/Gray Piotr was *pretending* he'd thought ahead, which would mean . . .

She thrust away all thoughts of court intrigue before they made her head burst. Better to concentrate on the grand ball to come.

Matt Hunter came out of the Metro station at Dupont Circle to find Leif already waiting for him.

"Hey!" Matt said, giving his pal a friendly punch in the shoulder, "been a while since I saw you. Thought you were going to spend all your time in New York City this summer."

Leif shrugged. "Mom headed back to Europe with some friends. Dad's down here in D.C. right now working on some sort of intense negotiations. It's all a very hush-hush deal. He won't talk about it, not even to me. I figured I'd come down, keep him company, and catch up with some of my friends."

Then it was Matt's turn to shrug. "You want to catch up with me, I can do it fast—not much is going on. It's been a pretty quiet summer down here. Hot, mainly. Except for sweating a lot, I don't have anything to report. How about you?"

"Let's see." Leif screwed his face into a look of deep concentration. "Since finishing that summer course that Andy sabotaged for me, I nearly got whacked by a robber, survived a duel, helped wreck a couple of nasty political intrigues, and unmasked a traitor in the palace guard."

Matt stared for a moment, his eyes going wide. Then he began to laugh. "That crazy sim! Lithuania, or whatever they call it."

"Latvinia," Leif corrected him.

Matt shook his head. "Yeah. I've heard a lot about it. In our crew—the Net Force Explorers especially—people are either crazy for it . . . or they're being driven crazy *by* it."

"Megan, P.J., and David are really talking it up that much?" Leif said.

"Not so much David—that's not his style," Matt replied. "But P.J. obviously thinks it's the coolest thing since indoor plumbing. And from the way she's been talking about it, I think Megan is beginning to believe she really is a princess."

Leif winced. "Ooh, I could see that happening. How about the rest of you guys—the unbelievers?"

"I can take it or leave it," Matt admitted. "The Squirt

won't even talk about it. He tried to get in, but got bounced because of his age."

That got a laugh out of Leif. "The Squirt" was Mark Gridley, son of the Net Force director. Mark was a computer wizard and a Net Force Explorer, but very young, only thirteen years old.

"I figured he'd be telling everybody he could design a better sim," Leif said.

"Nope, he just iced it out," Matt said. "Maj Greene has started ducking whenever she sees Megan. She says this sim is like a long, boring flatfilm—only it's worse because people you know are in it."

"I would think Andy would be having a field day with this turn-of-the-century stuff," Leif said. "Asking Megan if she wears a bustle on her butt, that kind of stuff."

"Not anymore," Matt said, shaking his head. "The last time he goofed on Lith—Latvinia, Megan acted as if she were going to challenge him to a duel."

Leif jammed his hands in his pockets and laughed. "She might do just do that, too. Fencing and Latvinia seem to be the two things she's doing this summer." He rolled his eyes. "Some people take things too seriously. They start to think virtual reality is *reality.*"

"And you don't?" Matt asked.

"I can take Latvinia or leave it," Leif told him.

"I thought that would be your thing," Matt said. "Hauling out your trusty sword and charging around with it."

"The place can pop some nasty surprises on you." Leif's hands clenched into fists for a second as he remembered some of them. "In my case, they seem to crawl out of the woodwork the moment I happen to touch the hilt of my sword."

"Doesn't sound like a lot of fun," Matt said. "David

didn't sound exactly wild about the place, either."

Leif shrugged.

Matt grinned. "On the other hand, Captain Winters is delighted that you and Megan are so into this Latvinia place."

Captain James Winters was the liaison agent between Net Force and the Net Force Explorers. "Winters likes it?" Leif said in disbelief.

"He said it's kept two of his biggest headaches—you and Megan—too busy to create any trouble for him this summer." Matt laughed. "At least, so far."

"I think he should pay more attention," Leif said. "There's some exposure possible if something goes wrong on the beta test. Besides us regular Net Force Explorers, he's got a Senator's son in Latvinia—not to mention the Russian ambassador's kid."

All this mentioning of Latvinia got Leif glancing at his watch. This was about the time he usually synched in with his computer, opening the cybergate to Latvinia. There was a royal ball that evening . . . but nothing important happening this afternoon.

Leif hesitated for just a moment, then slapped Matt on the back. "Enough of this Latvinia crap," he said decisively. "That's not what I came to Washington for. Let's have fun."

He grinned as he and Matt left the central traffic island, crossing the street. "What's doing around here in real life?" Leif asked. "Think we could find ourselves a baseball game?"

Leif got home later than he'd planned that evening. He'd already checked in by phone and gotten the message from his dad. The super-secret business negotiations were going to continue over supper. Leif unlocked the apartment door to the Andersons' Washington *pied à terre* and zipped straight to the kitchen. Given the family's often weird schedules, the freezer was always stocked with dinners to be nuked.

Sniffing appreciatively as a nice beef dish began to bubble in the cooker, Leif rummaged around for a plate and silverware. This wasn't some mass-produced glop prepackaged in a food factory. The Andersons could pay for real people to prepare real food. Nowadays, it seemed to Leif that commercial frozen food sometimes tasted faintly of fish oil—even when the dish was supposed to be meat. Probably just his imagination—or maybe it was that heart-healthy stuff the government had added to any high-cholesterol meal.

The oven bleeped, signaling that its heating job was done. Leif removed his dinner, juggling the hot container until he got it emptied onto his plate. Then, blowing on each forkful, he began shoveling the food into his mouth.

There was supposed to be a big feast during the ball tonight. One of the big nightmares about the Net had been the specter of people jacked into fantasy worlds, forgetting reality for so long that they starved to death.

Built-in safety features would keep that from happening, but there was a big difference between starvation and missing a meal. On the other hand, Leif knew from personal experience that eating virtual food instead of the real thing would leave him with a ravenous case of the munchies when he synched out. Better to feed his face now than wait until later and get socked.

He took another look at his watch. There was still a little time before the ball was supposed to begin. All he'd miss would be the boring last-minute preparations—hair-combing and so on. Leif finished his hurried meal at the kitchen counter, washing it down with a glass of juice. Then he washed his dishes, made a quick pit stop in the john, and headed down the hall to his bedroom.

The computer-link chair by the window here was the same top-of-the-line model as the one back home. Leif bypassed it to set the room's air-conditioner for low— no sense freezing in reality while he was in Latvinia. Then he took a moment or two to carefully calibrate the chair. It had been a while since he'd used it, and he didn't want to be dealing with implant pains when he arrived at the ball.

That should do it, he thought, finishing his minute adjustments. He settled back into the comfortable upholstery, let his eyelids come together, and gave a mental command to synch straight into Latvinia.

Leif opened his eyes to find himself walking down a palace corridor.

Nice to know I'm on time, he thought, pausing for a second to lean against the tapestry-covered wall and let the brief twinge of static in his implants die away. *I'm already on my way to the ball.*

Leif looked down at the conservative uniform he'd chosen to wear tonight. No super-tight riding pants tucked into tall boots this evening. He was wearing a dress uniform military tunic and gray trousers with gold piping down the seams. The jacket was bloody-nose red, with enough gold braid worked into the chest to qualify as light armor.

I wonder if the girls will find it scratchy when I dance with them, he thought.

Instead of boots, he had on lightweight dancing shoes. And, of course, there was the ceremonial sword at his side. That might make for a bit of a handicap while he was swirling around on the dance floor.

Satisfied by his brief inspection that the sim had taken care of all the necessary preparations for his appearance at the ball—he backed the inspection up by a quick look in a wall mirror—Leif continued on to the royal ballroom. Several harassed-looking flunkies, dressed in even louder silk outfits and larger powdered wigs than those he'd seen previously, stood outside the door.

One carried an ornate wooden staff with silver fittings. "Sir," the head flunky said in tones of rebuke, "Her Majesty will appear in moments."

"Then I suppose you'd better announce me immediately," Leif replied in his haughtiest tones.

The doors flew open, and the lead flunky stepped inside, thumping the staff on the floor. "The baron Albrecht von Hengist," he called out.

Leif stepped into the ballroom, to find himself confronted with a much more colorful assemblage than he'd expected. The ladies' gowns were even more flamboyant now than they'd been during the day, colorful concoctions of silk and lace that showed off shapely bare shoulders and a king's ransom worth of jewels. Apparently every male with any kind of military connection had a dress uniform of some sort and had dragged it out for the occasion. No two seemed to be the same, and Leif's crimson-and-gold number seemed quiet and tasteful compared to some of the getups around him.

If I really wanted to stand out around here, I should have worn a nice, simple black-and-white tuxedo, Leif thought as he walked through the thronged nobility. No, this ball was white tie. He'd need to wear a formal cutaway coat here, and he hated those things. The tails always made him feel like Jiminy Cricket. He imagined that the historical version of the rig would be even more uncomfortable than the modern version. He was glad he'd stuck with his uniform.

Leif caught a familiar face in the crowd. David Gray stood impassively in gorgeous silk robes, with a uniformed P.J. standing beside him. Actually, P.J. was chatting with three or four court cuties while David pretended to pay no attention to the by-play.

"Hey, there, baron," P.J. called out, doing his best imitation of a Texan abroad. "Thought you were going to miss this hoedown. Were you visiting your old girlfriend in the hospital?"

"What? Who? Where?" Leif asked.

"You didn't hear?" P.J. chuckled. "Your lady friend—Violin or whatever she calls herself—tried to stir up the peasants again. This time she didn't get dumped in horse flop. She was wavin' the red flag of revolution—literally, ya' know—and darned if a lightning bolt didn't come down and get her—*ka-ZAP!*"

"Frankly, I thought her speeches were electrifying enough," David said dryly. "Apparently, the monarch really does rule by divine right around here."

"I'm afraid no one told me about this," Leif said. It sounded as though the Latvinia program had some serious responses built in to deal with people who tried to mess with the basic concepts of the sim.

"Guess you were gettin' duded up for tonight's wingding." P.J. grinned broadly. "At least you didn't turn up in your nightshirt like Prince Menelik, here."

"Consider it antidancing insurance," David replied. Leif knew his friend enjoyed modern dances, but apparently David wasn't so sure of the more formal dance steps of the 1900s. And given David's previous experience with the program's lack of backup knowledge he'd run into so far, he clearly wasn't taking any chances.

"Don't be so sure of that," P.J. cracked. "Some girls might be willing to take a spin with you just to find out what you're wearing under that getup."

David turned away with a billow of silk.

If his complexion were as fair as mine, I suspect he'd be blushing right now, Leif thought.

Luckily, P.J.'s teasing was ended when the head flunky again came through the double doors to thump his staff. "Her Most Serene Majesty, the Princess Gwenda," the bewigged announcer called out.

All conversation ceased as everyone in the room went into a bow or curtsy.

Leif found himself staring as Megan came sweeping into the ballroom. Was it just an inspired combination of hairstyle, makeup, and fashion that made her look the way she did in the deceptively simple white gown set off with rubies? Or was the Latvinia program adding a little glamour to its star player?

There was no way that Leif could answer the question. All he knew was that he found himself moving across the ballroom like an iron filing attracted by a magnet.

Megan was going through the usual excruciating royal formalities. When she saw Leif, she extended her hand. He made a sweeping bow, kissing the back of her white glove.

"Baron," she said in a clear voice, "the festivities will not begin until I lead the first dance. Will you stand up with me?"

"Your Majesty, it would be an honor," Leif managed to say without tripping over his own tongue.

He took Megan in his arms in the most proper manner, and the strains of a waltz began to ring out over the room.

"I figured that snob school your parents send you to

would have taught you how to do this the right way," Megan whispered as they sailed across the floor. "I need all the help I can get to pull this off." All around them, other couples began to dance—with varying degrees of ability, Leif had to admit. He and Megan were acquitting themselves well.

His eyes were suddenly drawn to a dark spot in the colorful crowd. Alan Slaney had chosen a uniform of almost charcoal gray. The only trace of color in his outfit was a crimson sash across his chest. It made him look as if someone had slashed him from shoulder to hip.

Alan's—or Gray Piotr's—face was as expressionless as a statue's. But his eyes seemed to be tracking Megan and Leif as they danced.

Watch this, then, Leif thought, trying a twirl and a spin from his much-despised society dance lessons.

Megan laughed as they carried it off. "So, I guess the old saying is true," she said. "The best swordsmen *do* make the best dancers."

"You're not doing so badly yourself, for imitation royalty," Leif replied.

"That's just martial arts training, with a little assist from this program, not inbred grace," Megan told him. "But I admit I'm having fun. Let's try that move again— now that I'm ready for it."

It was a good evening. After his dance with Megan, the ladies of the court fluttered around Leif like a cloud of brightly colored butterflies. He danced, flirted just a bit, enjoyed the champagne, ate his way through a sumptuous feast . . . and soon enough headed for his bedroom in the royal tower, where he could synch out and rejoin the real world without paying for his virtual excesses.

Maybe it was because he'd been to actual parties like

this one that the whole ball scene didn't have quite the effect on him that it seemed to be having on everyone else.

Or maybe he left early because he knew that royal tradition limited guests to one dance per evening with any member of the royal family.

In any event, Leif was alone as he threaded his way through the maze of passages to the stairs that led to his apartment well before midnight. He moved quietly, not wanting to draw attention to himself or his early departure. He steadied his saber against his leg as he headed up. It hadn't succeeded in tripping him up while he'd been dancing, but he didn't want the scabbard banging against the walls as he went up the spiral staircase.

That's when he noticed the figure ahead of him. At first, he took it for a servant. But why would a servant be shrouded in a heavy black cloak indoors?

Maybe it could be some sort of monk. He'd noticed that religious people in Latvinia all wore costumes with hoods or cowls. But there were no guests that he knew of besides his friends staying in the tower, and that included monks.

Only when the climber reached the second floor and stepped out, checking that the way was clear, did Leif catch the glint of light coming off whatever the mystery figure was carrying.

The gleam was in the wrong place for a glass or a bottle. It was the wrong color, too. What he'd seen was the glint of candlelight off polished metal.

Leif hurtled up the stairs. Unless he missed his guess, that cloaked person held a drawn knife—which meant that the stranger was no servant or monk, but a potential assassin!

9

"Stop right there!" Leif roared, pulling out his saber and charging up the stairs.

Of course, the intruder did no such thing. In a swirl of cloak, he darted through the doorway leading to the second floor.

Leif was right behind him.

He's got a knife, I've got a sword, Leif thought. *That gives me the reach on him.*

Extending his sword, Leif moved forward to attack. But as he closed on the figure, he found that the cloak had hidden more than the assassin's identity. The man whipped up a long sword from beneath black wool garment.

Leif skidded to a stop just short of impaling himself. His opponent now held a sword—an old-fashioned rapier—extended in his right hand, with a dagger held low in his left hand. The guy looked like an illustration from a book on Renaissance swordfighting. But he also looked only too competent with his chosen tools.

People had generally stopped using those big cut-and-thrust swords by the 1700s, Leif thought. The rapier was heavier and more unwieldy than his saber. It was also a good four inches *longer*—something he'd have to remember in finding his distance.

Stepping quickly to the side and out of range, Leif pulled a small tapestry down from the wall, wrapping it around his left arm. He'd need the padding to help protect himself against that other blade, and he'd seen this trick used in historical adventure holos.

The only problem was that Leif didn't exactly know how to use his improvised defense, while his opponent was obviously a pro.

Can't let him set the rules, Leif told himself, popping in for a quick slash while bringing his tapestry-shielded arm up to cover his chest.

The assassin didn't respond with the back-and-forth moves Leif was familiar with from the fencing strip. Instead, his opponent sidestepped, circling, the tip of his blade coming over the top of Leif's wrapped arm. Cold steel sliced through gold brocade of Leif's uniform tunic, leaving a small, shallow cut under the right side of Leif's collarbone.

Leif gave a little yip of pain and stepped back. His adversary kept moving in a deadly crouch, constantly shifting the positions of his two blades, sometimes leading with the sword, sometimes with the foot-long dagger. His obvious skill and speed only added to Leif's misery.

Physically, Leif was okay. This was veeyar, after all, and he kept his pain thresholds set at conservative levels back in the real world. But the consequences of the cut were real enough in veeyar—and would soon affect his ability to perform well in the sim if he'd sustained enough damage. The little nick he'd taken stung like anything, but as far as he could tell in the bloodred tunic, it wasn't really bleeding—at least, he hoped not. But Leif was frankly rattled at how easily the guy had touched him.

Got to be careful, he thought, watching the smooth, quick movements of his opponent's two blades. The point of that long rapier seemed almost alive, questing around in front of his face. *Be* very *careful*, he reminded himself.

Sweat must be leaking into that little cut. The stinging was getting even worse. And the last thing Leif needed right now was a distraction.

There! Was that an opening? Leif tried to seize the initiative with another attack. The assassin's rapier parried Leif's blow, while simultaneously his dagger streaked for Leif's stomach.

Again, Leif was forced to backpedal before the guy sliced him a fresh belly button. That hadn't been an opening, it had been an invitation, suckering Leif in.

Leif was suddenly reminded of his disastrous duel with the hard-faced Frenchman.

Oh God, it's happening again. I've really stepped in it this time, Leif thought, watching his opponent's sword advance, then pull back while the dagger came forward. *And it's pretty damned deep.*

He saw another possible opening, but shook his head. Another trap. The assassin's style seemed based on the idea of preempting any attack with an even more aggressive move. Leif wasn't eager to fool with that hairtrigger again—at least not by himself.

"Ah—guards?" he called, trying to keep the desperate tone out of his voice. "Guards? Is there a guard around? I could really use one right now."

No answer—unless you counted the fact that the assassin was pressing Leif much harder. Apparently, the passive testing—offering openings—was over. Now the man's two blades were attempting to get through Leif's defenses—his shorter sword and the fabric wrapped around his left forearm.

It was like a nightmare! Leif couldn't even engage his opponent's blade. Whenever he tried to put his saber against that damned rapier, the assassin's blade somehow eluded him, always coming back in line to attack.

The point bored in again, and Leif tried a circular parry, hoping to deflect the rapier while bringing his own point into position to attack.

It was as if the intruder were reading his mind. Their blades never touched, the rapier's point moving in a counter-circle to keep Leif in danger.

The nick Leif had taken felt as if someone were dabbing it with acid. Could the point of his opponent's sword be smeared with poison? No, it was just good, honest sweat, pouring down his chest—and unintentionally rubbing salt in his wound. That was the least of Leif's problems. Sooner or later one of the attacker's weapons would penetrate Leif's defense. And that meant that shortly, Leif himself would be penetrated by either forty or twelve inches of cold steel. Each time he managed to evade an attack, his adversary was moving in, the point of the rapier coming closer, and closer, and closer.

Every instinct was screaming at him to run, but there was no way he could turn his back on this killer, even in veeyar. He tried a desperate improvisation, unwrapping some of the tapestry around his left arm and flapping it in the assassin's face.

Maybe I can put a little distance between us, Leif thought just as he collided with an old wooden chair.

Every once in a while a thronelike chair or heavy trestle table was stationed along the corridors, maybe for variety in the scenery. It was just Leif's bad luck to blunder into one of them now.

The assassin leaped forward to finish the fight.

A blast of thunder nearly deafened Leif. But he wasn't so out of it not to notice his attacker suddenly flying back, tumbling like a marionette with all its strings cut.

Leif glanced over his shoulder to see Sergei Chernevsky. The Russian boy was in his usual Hussar's uniform, but instead of his sword, he held a huge, old-fashioned revolver. That was the source of the roar that had nearly taken out Leif's eardrum. "What—" he began.

"I took the guard duty tonight," Sergei explained. "I get to see enough diplomatic balls. Maybe I find something more interesting, instead." He gestured toward the flattened assassin. "Like this."

Saber back at the ready, Leif approached the man in the black cloak. The rapier lay a foot from one hand, the dagger even farther away. His former adversary didn't look as though he'd be getting up anytime very soon.

Leif kicked the weapons out of reach, then cautiously prodded the prostrate form. The cloak shifted, revealing a neat hole in the intruder's chest. Leif didn't want to see where the bullet came out. Probably not a pretty sight.

The excess of adrenalin still humming through Leif's veins had him turning on Sergei. "What did you go and kill him for?" Leif shouted. "Now we'll never find out who sent him!"

"I thought I was saving your life," the Russian boy replied simply.

"Oh," Leif said. Undoubtedly true. Still—"Couldn't you have wounded him?"

Sergei gave him a look. "Or maybe knocked both weapons from his hands with a pair of shots?" He gestured with the heavy horse pistol. "What I have here is more like a cannon than a real gun, my friend. I count myself lucky I hit him instead of you."

The clumping of heavy boots echoed up the stairway. At least the guards on the other floors had heard Sergei's shot, even if they hadn't noticed Leif's life-and-death fight.

Leif was still suffering from the aftereffects of his battle. His hand was trembling so badly that it took three tries before he could sheathe his saber.

He shook his head. Clashing blades were all very fine in competitions with rules or in holo or in literature. But this hadn't even been steel to steel dueling—just a silent, murderous attempt to turn Leif into mincemeat. Tonight he'd almost been exiled from Latvinia—in about the hardest way he could imagine.

Leif clenched his hands, trying to still them. He'd joked about what seemed to happen to him whenever he touched a sword in Latvinia. But it really began to seem as though the sim was as hostile to him as it had been to Roberta Hendry.

He pushed that thought aside as he turned to Sergei. "Do you think we can keep this quiet for the time being?" he said as royal guardsmen appeared from the stairway. "It's not just that we'd be breaking up the party downstairs—some people might get ideas if they heard about an assassin being stopped this close to the royal apartments."

Sergei ran an eye over the arriving military men. "No problem," he assured Leif. "Most of these, I think, are nonrole-playing characters. Everybody who wants to be anybody was going to the ball tonight."

He touched the insignia at this throat, "In any event, I outrank them. Let's see what can be done."

Leif figured that any statements that had to be made could be taken care of the next day. Sergei accompanied him up to his room, but even so he cautiously peered into shadows and checked out dark doorways all along the route. Once he was safely locked in, Leif synched out. Then he sat up on his computer-link couch, stretched, and headed immediately for a shower. He no longer had the nick under his clavicle, but his clothes were drenched with cold sweat.

Even though he could barely keep his eyes open, he knew that dried sweat would itch like crazy all night if he didn't deal with it. Leif went to bed, tossing and turning from an unending stream of nightmares.

In the worst of them, he faced the murderous assassin again. But this time the ever-moving blade of the killer's rapier didn't just move as if it were alive. It *was* alive, turning into a poisonous cobra which leaped and bit him right under the collarbone. . . .

Leif found himself half out of bed after that one, his head on the floor, both hands clutching at his chest. His heart was pounding as if he'd run up the stairs to the top of the Washington Monument.

"Don't know which is worse," he mumbled, stumbling for the bathroom. "Slaney's goofball veeyar creation, or the sims my own subconscious is sticking me with."

One thing was sure. He literally had Latvinia on the brain. Leif looked at the clock, shook his head, and padded down the hallway to the kitchen.

His father was just finishing breakfast as Leif came in—he was eating doctor-approved cereal and skim milk instead of the bacon and eggs Magnus Anderson preferred. Leif sniffed the air, but it seemed there was no coffee for him to wake up and smell.

Magnus Anderson held out the cup in his hand. "Tea," he said with some disgust. "The latest advice from my doctor. I'm not sure the stress of deprivation and caffeine addiction isn't doing more damage than good."

"I need more of a caffeine jolt," Leif said, making a beeline for the coffeemaker, where he gathered together the makings of a full pot.

"You were in bed early enough—tucked in by the time I got home," Leif's father said. "Although I know you consider anything shy of eight-thirty in the morning uncomfortably close to dawn, you should have gotten a decent night's sleep. What's up?"

"Nightmares," Leif replied, regretting it even as the word left his lips. "I had a pretty intense sword fight in Latvinia last night, and I relived it—with worse details— in my sleep."

"When veeyar first came in, a lot of people were afraid that would happen to their children—the little ones would be too stimulated." Magnus Anderson gave his son a dubious look. "I never heard you complain about such a thing before." He hesitated. "If this sim is upsetting you, maybe it would be just as well if you stayed out of it."

Leif shook his head. "I'm not going to let a bunch of

electrons scare me away," he said. "Besides, there are real-life consequences to consider. Megan O'Malley would skin me alive if I pulled out now."

His father shook his head. "Your most dependable motive," he said in a dry voice. *"Cherchez la femme."*

That was actually a popular French line—"search for the woman." Leif didn't know how to interpret or answer that, but luckily he was spared. Magnus Anderson glanced at his watch and put his cup down. "Early morning meetings." He sighed. "Do you mind dealing with these dishes before your mother sees them?"

Leif shrugged. "I'll take care of them. Don't worry about it, Dad," he said. "Look on the bright side. With luck, they may drag you off to a power breakfast at that meeting of yours."

His father grinned. "I can only hope so. It would be rude of me to refuse such hospitality."

Leif saw his father out the door, returned to the kitchen, and poured himself a cup of coffee. The refrigerator was noticeably lacking in the makings of a hearty breakfast—clearly Dad was trying to avoid temptation—but Leif dug out some frozen egg whites. Adding chopped scallions and a heaping helping of ham bits, Leif constructed a reasonable omelet. There was fresh bread in the refrigerator, so he had toast. Washed down with a couple of cups of coffee—not to mention a generous dollop of catsup, the meal went down easily enough.

Leif spent a while fumphing around the apartment, catching snatches of several morning holonews programs, checking the weather, walking around. He couldn't seem to sit down and pay attention to anything.

Finally he took another shower, dressed, and looked at the clock. Maybe it was a little early—

Leif shook his head and went to the computer-link couch. He lay back, experienced the usual disorienting buzz between the ears, and opened his eyes in Latvinia. Apparently the Baron Albrecht von Hengist was an early riser today, too. Leif's virtual self was washed, shaved, and dressed—in a more informal uniform today. There was no trace of breakfast in the room, but Leif pushed that thought away. Instead, he went to the writing desk and dashed off a couple of notes. Then he rang for a servant.

"Please deliver these to the princess and the prime minister," he said to the valet who appeared.

"Sir—Her Majesty requested your presence as soon as you were available," the uniformed flunky replied.

Instead of being herded to the throne room, Leif was led upstairs to the royal apartments. Megan met him in a book-lined study. Sitting with her was the Graf von Esbach.

"It seems we owe you another debt, Baron," the prime minister said. "Had you not apprehended that assassin, last night's festivities might have ended very differently."

Leif raised an eyebrow. "I'm afraid I was merely offering the fellow some healthful exercise," he said. "Young Chernevsky was the one who ended the menace."

"By ending the intruder's life." Von Esbach shook his head. "I would give a great deal to have that fellow alive and talking."

Megan finally spoke up. "I only learned of these events this morning." She surprised Leif by acting like a turn-of-the-century heroine, taking his hands and leaning forward.

"No harm done, Your—"

"I got an urgent priority message on my system, from our friend Alan," she said to Leif in a low voice. "Not good. I am *not* a morning person."

"I had hoped you wouldn't hear anything until I could investigate," Leif began.

"Quite impossible," von Esbach interrupted, giving Leif a fishy look. "Colonel Vojak was quite annoyed that you tried to cover up the affair. Especially considering your friendship with that anarchist."

"Miss Gamba?" Leif said in puzzlement. "What connection could there possibly be—"

"Anarchist literature was found on the dead man's person," the prime minister said solemnly. "I regret to say that the news has apparently leaked to the public at large. There is only one anarchist of note at large in Latvinia. I fear a good many people believe last night's attack was instigated by Miss Gamba."

"That's—" Leif bit off the rather vulgar word he'd been about to use. "Ridiculous," he finally said. "We don't even know who was the fellow's target."

Who *had* the black-cloaked figure been after? Was the assassin aiming for the ailing king? Had he intended to ambush Megan? Or had this fencing wizard appeared merely to make Leif's life miserable?

"As for Miss Gamba, however one might disagree with her politics, she has certainly conducted all her activities in the open," Leif went on. "To accuse her of conspiracy—"

He was interrupted by applause from the doorway. How long had Alan Slaney been standing there? "It is most gallant of you to defend your friend," Gray Piotr said. "However, we must face facts. With the amount of bad feeling against the young lady, we cannot guarantee her safety in Latvinia."

Alan, in his role as Gray Piotr, nodded to von Esbach. "I've sent a detachment of soldiers to bring her from the hospital to the palace. However, as soon as we can arrange it, a special train should take her out of the country."

The prime minister nodded. "Mob violence can be an ugly thing."

"I believe our guest has even now arrived," Gray Piotr turned back to the doorway. A squad of soldiers in plain gray and green marched in, surrounding a stretcher detail. Reclining on the stretcher was Roberta Hendry. She still seemed half-paralyzed after her brush with the lightning bolt. But her eyes blazed with fury.

"This isn't over," the dark-haired girl croaked.

"It's only for your own safety, dear woman," Gray Piotr said. "Heaven forfend that anything worse happen to you in our little land."

In a more businesslike tone he asked the officer in charge, "Has the train been prepared?"

"Sir, it should be ready soon," the soldier replied.

"Excellent." The man who would be king turned to Megan. "Cousin? I realize my actions might seem high-handed. But I think they're preferable to riot—and murder."

Megan nodded uncomfortably. Gray Piotr linked arms with the prime minister. "Von Esbach, perhaps you should come along to make sure all the legalities are attended to."

Leif and Megan watched the small parade move off.

As soon as they were alone, Megan burst out, "Can you figure out what's going on there?"

"More important, do you think that your friend Alan knows what he's doing?" Leif asked. "He can try humiliating and shutting her up here in Latvinia, but Roberta has serious juice out in the real world. Her parents know half the movers and shakers in Washington, and that includes plenty of bigwigs at AHSO. If she lodges a complaint—"

"What?" Megan demanded. "They can't pull the plug on the sim."

"But they could change the rules for all the Special Interest Group members," Leif replied. "They could declare Latvinia off-limits for AHSO members. That would be one easy way to end the beta-test. Alan would have no customers. He'd have no way of getting a payoff for all the time he's put in."

"Look—I don't know what's going on here." Megan was definitely getting upset. "But I'm sure, whatever it is, it's going on to further the plot."

"Yeah," Leif said, "Sure." Considering Megan's worried mood, he didn't add what he wanted to say.

The question is, he thought, *whose plot are we talking about?*

IO

"Ouch!" Megan O'Malley yelped as her opponent's blade whacked her right in the midriff. She stepped back, lowering her own saber as her free hand rubbed at her "wound." That hurt, even through several layers of padded fencing jacket.

"Reverse moulinet." Her opponent remained on guard. And Megan wasn't sure, but she suspected he was grinning behind his fencing mask.

What made things worse, this was the balding, out-of-shape guy who usually couldn't touch her. But then, that was the way the whole evening's practice had gone. People had criticized her during the exercises, then picked on her during the free bouting section. And she wasn't holding her own, so she could hardly blame them for it.

Taking a deep breath, Megan brought her sword up,

assumed the *en garde* position, and said, "Let's go."

She did all right for a couple of minutes, and then, humiliatingly, the guy nailed her again!

"Megan!" Alan Slaney called. "Could I see you, please."

She went through the after-bout ritual—saluting, removing her mask, and shaking hands with her opponent—even though what she really wanted to do was punch in his face. Then she walked over to where Alan stood observing the room with his back to a wall.

"What's wrong?" Alan asked.

"Nothing," Megan answered. "Absolutely nothing."

"Megan, I've been watching you tonight. Maybe you think you're trying, but you're just going through the motions. And when that happens, you get results like Ed there trouncing you. Alan shook his head. "Whether you want to admit it or not, there's some sort of distraction coming between you and your fencing. And until you deal with whatever is bothering you, you might as well hang a big sign on your chest that says, 'Please beat me up!' Because that's what every fencing partner you face will do."

"There is something wrong," Megan confessed. "Something about Latvinia. But you said we're not supposed to talk about it in the salle."

"That's just to keep people from getting distracted. But if it's making you fence like you're sleepwalking, maybe we'd *better* talk about it," Alan said. "I know your character has more duties than you might have expected. Is this about being virtmailed so early this morning?"

Megan shook her head. "It's about what happened after. That girl, Roberta Whatsername. Leif knows her. He says she's not going to take being thrown out of the sim lying down."

Alan grinned. "That's about all she could do, after being struck by lightning."

"That's not all she can do out here in real life," Megan explained. "Her Mumsy and Pater aren't your ordinary set of parents. They've got endless resources. They also know everybody, and that apparently includes some of the muckety-mucks at AHSO."

"I'm well within my rights to boot her out. The responsible authority for any SIG or sim—which in this case is yours truly—is allowed to eject anyone whose activities demonstrably disrupt the basic concept agreed upon for simulation. Which is what Roberta was trying to do, starting the Russian Revolution about twenty years too early. It's in the AHSO bylaws, to prevent participants from imposing their particular view of history—you know, the folks who expect to find hidden Viking colonies in America, or who demand to see alien gods from space building the pyramids. They're free to develop their own alternative sims, but they aren't allowed to ruin the party for everybody else in one that's up and running according to a given set of rules."

"I know that," Megan said. "But there *were* anarchists in the period you're dealing with."

"And I arranged for Roberta to be treated much better than most governments of the day treated accused anarchists," Alan replied. "Would it have been better to stick her in a dungeon for the rest of the beta-test? Or have her hung or shot? Any of those actions would have been historically accurate."

"I don't know," Megan admitted. "But I do know this. Rules don't matter much to the rich and powerful. And Leif says that Roberta has the juice to turn AHSO against you at the national level. You've obviously worked so hard on Latvinia—I don't want to see it fail before it becomes a moneymaking proposition for you."

Alan shook his head. "I never went into the Latvinia project to make a profit," he said gently. "You might call it a labor of love."

"But it will be an empty labor if AHSO makes all its members pull out," Megan insisted. "And it seems Roberta might be able to make that happen."

"I think I can keep most of the adventurers." Alan sounded confident, but a little worried wrinkle appeared between his eyebrows. "All I need is a little time to work it through. But thanks for the warning, Megan. Thank Leif as well."

Leif cautiously checked out his virtmail, expecting to find some sort of flame job from Roberta Hendry. When he saw nothing, he was surprised . . . and somewhat curious. It was out of character for her.

"Computer," he ordered, "research function. Scan for mentions in the media regarding the Hendry family—specifically, Alexander Hendry, Susan Hendry, or Roberta Hendry."

That specified Roberta, her dad, and her mom, but was a bit too broad. He'd get blasted with information.

"Focus on society news," he added, "for the last four months. Execute."

"Searching," the computer's silver-toned voice responded.

Moments later the computer's holographic display began to fill with various references to the Hendry clan. Leif quickly weeded out stories about Roberta's attempts to bring back radical chic, or about Mrs. Hendry's home and garden tours. There were fewer references to the balls and parties the family would usually be gracing, then Leif saw why.

Alexander and Susan Hendry were apparently spending the summer at some count's villa in Monaco. It would make a nice vacation, but they wouldn't get the press among the international jet set that they would in their hometown papers.

"Too bad Roberta didn't choose to visit that little principality instead of Latvinia," Leif muttered as he looked through the rest of the clips. "Although they'd probably take much more practical action there if she tried to chain herself to the casino doors."

He told the computer to delete the references and plumped down on the living room couch. It looked like a dead night—nothing worth watching on the holo—or rather, if there was, it was just too much effort to search out. After his early morning, Leif didn't have the energy to find himself a party or hook up with anybody who wanted to go dancing. And with both Megan and Alan Slaney off at fencing practice, he was ready to bet that nothing exciting would be going on in Latvinia.

Right now the biggest danger threatening the kingdom was out here in real life. Would Roberta make good on her threats?

Leif turned to the living room computer console, ordering it into telephonic mode. Then he hesitated. His first choice to talk things over would be David—Leif valued his friend's calm, analytical approach to problems. But David might see Roberta as the solution to a problem. He was obviously not in love with Latvinia. Although it had been a clever idea to make David an Abyssinian prince, that plot device had also made him a fish out of water in the Zenda-like setting.

P.J. Farris, on the other hand, was having a whale of

a time in the sim. It gave him the chance to shed the responsibilities of being a senator's son, kick back, and be as outrageous as he wanted to be.

And, Leif had to admit, Bronco Jack Farris was pretty outrageous as a rootin'-tootin' courtier. On one occasion he'd seen his friend give roping demonstrations by lassoing Megan's ladies in waiting, and then keep out of trouble by buttering the ladies up with a combination of cornpone humor and cowboy charm. Judging by the ladies' delighted grins, it wasn't the first time he'd tried it.

Yeah, P.J. would be more concerned about the future of Latvinia. And maybe his political background would help him come up with some suggestion that Leif just couldn't see now to stop the incoming trouble before it got ugly. He gave his computer the order to connect with the Farris phone number.

P.J. himself picked up, his face breaking into a grin when he recognized his caller. "You feelin' about as bored as I do, champ? I tell ya, I'm hooked. Man, the hours just seem to stretch on forever when there's nothing good goin' on in Latvinia."

"I'm sure you could always go in there and impress some girl with your Ragtime Cowboy Joe act," Leif shot back.

P.J. looked pained. "I am basing my characterization on a noted actor, raconteur, and roper—even if he did come from Oklahoma instead of Texas—I'm sure you've heard of Will Rogers."

"Oh, right," Leif said, vaguely remembering the name. "The burlesque comedian."

"Vaudeville, not burlesque," P.J. corrected. "There's a difference. The girls didn't wear much in the way of clothes in Ziegfeld's Follies, but they kept them on."

P.J.'s joking mood vanished when he heard why Leif was calling, however. "Shut down Latvinia?" P.J.'s distress showed in his voice. "Why would anyone want to do that? I'm having the most fun I've ever had since learning to ride a horse. Megan is obviously having the time of her life being a princess. Everybody's enjoying it. Why should some sorehead come along and shut the sim down?"

In the face of such enthusiasm, Leif decided to keep quiet about his own reservations. Instead, he pointed out, "Maybe that sorehead got annoyed about losing her dress, being dumped in a pile of *merde,* and then struck by lightning and deported."

"Oh, come on!" P.J. protested. "That guy who runs the Dominions of Sarxos role-playing game does much worse stuff to people who try to mess around with his sim."

"Rod," Leif said. "Chris Rodrigues. But Sarxos has been running a long time, with enough paying customers to make Chris rich many times over. Alan Slaney is just getting Latvinia off the ground—and he's aiming it toward AHSO people. If AHSO pulls its members out, Latvinia crashes and burns."

"We can't let that happen." P.J. leaned toward the holo pickup, his face serious. "I mean, think how upset Megan would be."

Leif repressed a brief shudder at the thought. "That's why I'm talking to you instead of her. Megan would probably go over to Roberta's and put her in a choke-hold until she promised to lay off. I thought you might come up with a slightly more . . . political . . . solution."

P.J. just shook his head. "Most politicians I know would probably go for the choke-hold, too." He frowned, looking out at Leif. "Couldn't you just—well, *talk* to this Roberta person? Make her see how unfair she's being?"

Leif sighed. "Have you ever tried to get Megan to change her mind?"

P.J. nodded, wordless. But the look on his face told it all.

"Imagine that, *squared,* and backed up by a fortune and an 'I am bulletproof' attitude. Roberta's been given anything she ever wanted by her parents, and it shows in the worst way. She's not going to be rational. Megan's going to expect me to do something about it. And both Megan and Roberta have my phone number and Net addresses."

"So whatcha got here is a delicate decision, as far as you are concerned. Who is it that you really want to tee off? Roberta? Or Megan?"

Leif gave an unhappy nod. "That's it in a nutshell."

"I will say, Megan is likely to take it personal," P.J. went on. "And she's formidable. While this Roberta, despite her parents, sounds like the yelling kind. I'd plump for going up against Roberta. Just get yourself some good backup. Have you thought of asking Captain Winters for help here?"

"I'd have better luck getting the president lined up behind me," Leif replied. "We've got a history, you know. Winters doesn't exactly trust me."

"Well, I can't get you presidential backup, but I can offer some support from the Senate—at least from a senator's kid." P.J. grinned. "Think that might help turn this honey's head?"

"Maybe. It's a start," Leif admitted.

P.J. frowned in thought. "Suppose we get the guy who saved your bacon last night—Sergei. He's the son of the Russian ambassador." That big Texas grin came back.

"Create a sort of international peacemaking mission, y'know?"

"I don't know how to get hold of him," Leif said, "except that he's one of Alan Slaney's fencing students."

"Let me take care of that, then," P.J. promised. "Do you know where we can find this Roberta person? I figure we should get to work on her tomorrow morning."

Leif gave P.J. the Hendry address. "Just don't make it *too* early tomorrow morning," he said. "Roberta enjoys her sleep."

And so do I, he thought, as he signed. *It's one of the best parts of summer vacation. And I seem to have missed out on my share of it so far.*

The next morning Leif got out of a cab in one of the quieter side streets of Georgetown—a super-ritzy part of an extremely ritzy neighborhood. It was a few minutes before eleven, the time they'd agreed to meet. But Sergei Chernevsky was already there, waiting by the corner.

It took Leif an instant to recognize the Russian boy out of uniform and with a few years shaved off his virtual appearance. He still didn't know how P.J. had tracked Sergei down so quickly—or how he'd persuaded him to come along. But the closer Leif came to actually meeting Roberta, the more hopeless their mission seemed.

"No sword," Sergei said, finally recognizing Leif without his Albrecht von Hengist beard.

"And no gun," Leif replied with a grin. "Though we might wish we had one if Roberta decides to fly off the handle."

"Fly off—?" Sergei had to think for a moment to translate Leif's slang. "Oh, you mean she'll get angry.

Well, maybe P.J. brings one of his six-shooters." He did a thumb-and-finger imitation of a pistol.

"To change Roberta's mind, you'd probably do better with a thermonuclear bomb," Leif said.

A moment later, P.J. came walking up the block. Apparently he'd spent the night getting cold feet, too. His grin was all too obviously false as he greeted the other two. "Well, guys. Ready?"

"As we'll ever be," Leif said. "Prepare to charm the socks off her, Pretty Boy."

P.J. shot Leif a look. "Don't call me Pretty Boy."

Leif knew his friend was sensitive about his male-model good looks, especially now that they weren't hidden by his weather-beaten Bronco Jack persona. He also knew that unless he distracted P.J. from his nervousness, their attempt to change Roberta's mind was doomed before they even started. Roberta's car was parked in the circular driveway framing the three-tiered fountain in front of the house. She was home, apparently. It was to time to try their luck.

P.J. leaped up the steps of the house and rang the bell. He stood there for a moment as the others climbed up to join him, then rang the bell again.

No one answered the door. Nor did any faces appear in the curtained windows.

"You'd expect to see a mess of servants in a place like this," P.J. said, irritation entering his voice. "Think the bell is dead?"

The walls of the old house were too thick to let them hear anything, and heavy drapes muffled the windows. P.J. made a fist and began rapping on the door. "I know you said she slept late," he told Leif, "but this is overdoing it."

Sergei only shrugged. "I do not believe she is jacked

into Latvinia," he said. "I checked just moments ago."

"Maybe she decided to join her folks in Europe," Leif offered. "With Roberta—"

"Excuse me," a voice interrupted him.

Leif turned around to find a short, stout, gray-haired woman walking up the steps looking him up and down.

"We—ah, were hoping to find Miss Hendry in," Leif said. "But when we rang, we didn't get an answer, either from her or the staff—"

"Well, now, you wouldn't, since Mr. and Mrs. Hendry gave most of the staff the summer off," the stout lady replied with a faint trace of Irish brogue. "I'm only in to do the day cleaning and to take care of Miss Roberta." She frowned. "I've no idea why she shouldn't be answering the door, as I expected her to let me in. She should be up and hungry for her breakfast by now." The woman began rummaging in her purse and produced a key ring. "But I'll certainly be getting an answer for you gentlemen after I see her."

The three boys stepped aside as the cleaning lady swept past with all the presence of a duchess going to court. Sergei began pointing out the obvious. "Maybe Roberta just doesn't want—"

Now his words were interrupted—by a scream.

Leif flung himself at the door, which swung wide open—the cleaning lady hadn't fully closed it. Banshee screams echoed off the marble walls and floor of the reception hall. Toward the rear of the house rose the central staircase, where the cleaning woman huddled, still screaming.

Then Leif realized the woman was huddled over another figure lying on the floor, a pale, still figure with great legs peeping out from under a frilly nightgown.

It was Roberta Hendry, and she was unconscious—
Or worse!

"I can't believe what I'm hearing!" Megan stared in shock at Leif's image on the holo connection. "You mean Roberta fell down the stairs answering the doorbell while you were pressing it?"

"No, that's not what the doctors think," Leif replied. "It's something to do with bruises having formed already, and her skin showing how dehydrated she was. The emergency services people weren't talking much—they were busy rushing her over to George Washington University Hospital. But they did tell me she was most likely collapsed at the foot of the stairs for hours—maybe all night."

"Sounds like she's lucky to be alive," Megan said numbly.

"If you call being in a coma with a cracked skull

lucky." Leif's muttered response was half-drowned out by an ambulance siren in the background.

He must be calling from the hospital, she realized.

"Beats a broken neck," Megan finally managed.

That got a ghost of a smile from Leif. "Maybe. You don't think that string of bad luck she had in Latvinia leaked out into real life, do you?"

"Don't be silly," Megan replied, her voice a little sharper than she'd intended.

"At least they've got Roberta stabilized, but they have no idea when she'll come out of this. Her parents are coming home from Europe—" Leif grimaced. "And all I want to do right now is get the smell of hospital out of my nose."

He hesitated for a second, then said, "I'm down here with my dad, but he's busy with some big deal or other. You free to do anything?"

Megan shook her head. "I'm stuck here. It's my week to do the dreaded laundry—and with a family as large as ours, it really *is* the dreaded laundry. Then Alan asked me to link in early—what?" she asked at the look on Leif's face.

"You're going back into Latvinia after this?" Leif's expression was definitely disapproving.

"You make it sound as though we should establish a day of national mourning," Megan said. "I'm sorry for what happened to Roberta, but it's not as if she died or anything. And there's certainly no link to Latvinia. Why shouldn't we go on with the beta-test?"

Leif shrugged, but Megan knew she hadn't changed his mind. For that matter, why was she feeling so defensive about this?

"I know you'll do whatever you intend to do," Leif finally said. "I just feel it's . . . inappropriate. Wrong, somehow. Oh well, have fun with the laundry. I'll see you later."

Megan said goodbye and hung up the phone, vaguely disquieted by the conversation. Or maybe, she thought, it was the thought of the laundry she now had no excuse to put off that was bothering her. Shaking her head, she went off to deal with it.

Coming home to an empty apartment only intensified Leif's bad mood.

Nothing like being turned down when I ask someone out to make me feel lousy, he thought. *She'd rather do* laundry *than see me! And sitting around alone after-ward—that's just the icing on the cake.*

He went to the living room computer console and put in a call to David Gray.

David picked up in the hallway of his family's apart-ment. Judging from the hooting and hollering in the background, his little brothers were busily inventing an-other of their weird games. When Leif filled him in on what had happened to Roberta, David shook his head. "Nobody deserves to have that happen to them—even if they are a pain in the butt."

He gave Leif a sidewise glance. "Although I might have a little more sympathy for her than a few other people would."

"Tell me about it," Leif said sourly. "Megan's flying right back into Latvinia—after she finishes the family laundry."

"From washerwoman to princess—you can see why the place has its attractions for her." David shook his head. "It's not quite the same for me."

"Or for me," Leif agreed. "You think it's any fun having my rump handed to me whenever I cross swords with someone? I can understand why Roberta finally got hit with lightning—she was really trying to stand the sim on its head. But—"

"You really want to see something?" David interrupted. "Go to your computer link and jack in. I'll meet you at your room in the palace."

A little surprised, Leif got up, went to his room, and set up his computer-link couch. He lay back, closed his eyes, gave the command . . . and found himself in Latvinia. He was glad that the program usually integrated arriving role-players in neutral settings—walking down a palace hallway, for instance. It was a lot easier than opening his eyes to find himself on a horse—or fighting a duel.

This time Leif found himself at the writing desk in his apartment at the palace. He was biting the end of an old-fashioned dip-the-point-in-the-ink pen, looking over a letter covering the events at court—including a couple Leif personally hadn't been present to see.

At a knock from the door, Leif put down his pen and went to answer. David stood in the doorway, wearing distinctly more European clothes than he usually wore as Prince Menelik.

"So, what's up?" Leif asked.

Not exactly what you'd call old-fashioned eloquence, he thought critically. *In fact, it's almost babbling.* Leif felt weird, linking in to Latvinia after giving Megan a hard time about her decision to visit the sim.

"Just follow me," David said, wearing his most impenetrable poker face. "I thought we'd just take a stroll through the streets of Herzen."

"Sure." Leif hadn't really had a chance to explore the capital. It might be interesting to check the city out.

Starting from the mansion district around the palace,

they headed downhill to the city's ritzy carriage-trade stores. Leif walked along, taking in the various architectural styles of the buildings—and looking at the occasional pretty chambermaid sashaying by. So far, Herzen reminded him of one of those historical theme parks—just not quite so shiny and pastel. There were touches of reality; for instance, horses relieved themselves in the street frequently enough to make you watch where you were stepping.

Leif recognized the street where they'd chugged up to the palace in their vintage Mercedes. The boulevard wasn't as crowded as it had been during the impromptu parade. But there were plenty of citizens—busy burghers—moving around to shop or complete errands.

It's like watching an old-time photograph come to life, Leif thought as a carriage clattered by. *Or rather, one of the colored illustrations in an old book.*

They were perhaps halfway down the street when he noticed one of the coachmen turning away, flicking his hand in an odd gesture. The forefinger and pinkie seemed to point at them for a second, the two fingers in between held down with the thumb.

As the boys proceeded along to the less prosperous section of the shopping street, down the street, Leif caught more and more of those quick, surreptitious hand-flicks.

David glanced at him. "Beginning to notice, huh?"

"What—" Leif began.

David cut him off. "Do me a favor," he said. "Walk on ahead for a block or so." He turned away, apparently fascinated by something on display in a shop window.

Leif walked on alone, glancing around, using windows as mirrors. None of those odd signs.

A couple of minutes later David rejoined him. They

continued along. As the neighborhood got shabbier, more and more people shot them the hand gesture, some more overtly than others.

David stopped, thrusting out an arm. "The train station is over that way, along with the warehouse district—a perfect setup for dens of thieves, or headquarters for conspiracies."

What Leif noticed however, was how passers-by avoided the pointing hand—even across the street.

Abruptly turning away, David led them in a different direction. "Over here, we have a case of urban decay—a neighborhood that would have been nicer once upon a time. They still have a park in the middle of this square."

The houses had probably been minor mansions once upon a time, and were now cut up to provide homes for several families. The trees in the square could have done with pruning, and shoots of grass thrust their way through the thin gravel on the walks. But young mothers were taking advantage of the nice weather to take their babies for a walk. Often they were accompanied by older women in head-scarves—babushkas. No one seemed to meet their gaze—but almost everyone was shooting that odd sign. If they weren't doing that, mothers and grandmothers were rearranging the kids' clothing.

David took Leif once around the park. Wherever they went, happy chattering in the peasant dialect went silent. One little guy, maybe three years old, came running along, playing some game. When he spotted David, he stopped in his tracks, staring up at David. A mother swooped down on him, hustling him away. As she nearly dragged the kid off, Leif saw one hand set in the odd sign. The other held up a scrap of red ribbon pinned to little one's collar.

"Two for two," David muttered, heading away. Leif

marched along in silence until they were halfway up the high street again.

"Okay," he finally said. "What was that all about?"

"I began wondering, too, after I noticed it happening a lot," David said pleasantly. "Had a heck of a time looking it up. It appears to be a genuine aversion sign, known in Italian as the *corno*—the horns. It's supposed to keep away the nastier side of supernatural life, like a rabbit's foot, or those little red ribbons you noticed on the kid. They neutralize the evil eye, or keep demons at bay."

"Demons?" Leif repeated a little stupidly.

"You know." David held out one hand and rubbed the back of it vigorously. "Doesn't rub off."

"Uh, well, uh—" Leif fumbled for a minute. "I suppose that's pretty authentic. Nasty, but realistic. The farther down the road we went, the more peasants we saw. And peasants in the Balkan back in the 1900s would probably never have encountered a black person—"

"Oh, I figured all that out, thanks." David's voice was sharp. "And it would be an authentic West Texas reaction for P.J. to call me 'boy,' too."

Leif stared. "P.J. would never—none of those people—I mean, they had to be nonrole-playing characters." He finally gave up explaining what David knew all too well.

"Yeah." David looked him straight in the eyes. "It would have to be part of the program. Maybe not as obvious as a lightning bolt or a sword in the face . . . just a subtle way to make sure I won't feel welcome in Latvinia."

They walked in silence back to the palace, Leif troubled, David just plain angry. When they came in view of the gates, one of the guards ran to intercept them.

"What now?" David muttered. "Do we have to go in by the back door?"

"S-sirs," the breathless guard stammered. "Her Majesty and the prime minister request your presence."

Megan and Graf von Esbach sat waiting for them in the same upstairs library/study where Roberta had been exiled. As Leif and David walked in, Megan looked up from the heavy oak table where she'd been resting her elbows. It was a beautifully carved piece of furniture, with shelves for books cut into either end. Sitting on the table, right between Megan's arms, was a gold chain. It held a diamond pendant, the stone about as large as the last joint of Leif's little finger.

"One of the crown jewels," Megan told him. "About ten carats."

Leif did the math with modern diamond prices and got a good-sized number in the six-figure range. "Nice."

Megan picked up a small bronze statue and brought it down heavily on the gemstone. When she lifted it up, there was only powder on the table. "Paste," she said conversationally. "Someone switched a fake for the real diamond."

David glanced shrewdly over at the Graf von Esbach. "And I suppose you don't need three guesses to pinpoint who's behind this."

The prime minister nodded. "I heard rumors that several disreputable types connected with Gray Piotr had been seen in the vicinity of the royal vault, and took it upon myself to investigate. Now I hear that one of Piotr's henchmen has set off for Vienna. If he were to dispose of several gemstones like this one, the Master of Grauheim would have sufficient ready money to hire himself an army."

"And stage his own *coup d'ètat*," Leif finished. He frowned. "Where can we find this henchman now?"

"He is out of the country," von Esbach said. "We have no legal way to detain him."

"But if he's in Vienna—" Fresh memories of Albrecht von Hengist called to Leif's attention, memories of disreputable characters he'd dealt with in the past. "I have certain connections there. The fellow might be found— and thwarted."

"Hold on," David suddenly said. "Time for a reality check. System, would this simulation actually allow a role-player to go to Vienna?"

A soft voice responded. "Negative. This simulation would calculate the time allowance for players traveling outside Latvinia, and arrange for an appropriate return. Actions taken outside of Latvinia would be resolved on a probability matrix—"

"That's enough, thanks," David interrupted. He shook his head in disapproval. "Not very slick designing. If you really wanted to factor in a plot twist like this, it wouldn't be that hard to program in the trip, condensing the time if necessary. I've done that myself for Mars voyages. It's kind of clunky to do it this way, running things like an old-time Dungeon Master with too many dice."

He frowned for a moment, then called on the system again. "Generate an estimate on how long players would have to be absent from Latvinia."

"Minimum journey and stay, seven to ten days," the computer replied.

David turned to Leif, one eyebrow raised, a lopsided smile on his lips.

What did he say? Leif thought. *Not as obvious as a lightning bolt?*

Still, Leif got the message.

"Well," he finally said. "When is the earliest we could set off?"

12

Megan felt her mouth drop open in a very un-princesslike gawk when she heard Leif's suggestion. It only got worse when David announced that he was ready to leave at once.

"What are you talking about?" she demanded. "I only showed you the false gems so we could discuss what to do about them!"

"I fear you were too dramatic, ma'am," Leif replied in his best turn-of-the-century style. "This is a development that should be investigated posthaste."

"You can't really be talking about leaving Latvinia!" Megan cried. "I won't have it! I won't allow it!"

"Won't allow it?" Leif repeated, slipping into a more modern idiom. "I think that wearing that crown may have cut off the flow of blood to your brain . . . Miss O'Malley."

David nodded. "This is the inner circle, remember? It's not a monarchy—just four people who happened to cross this border together. We'll put it up to a vote—if you get a majority, we'll stay."

Leif could only shrug helplessly. "At a quick count I'd say the numbers aren't on our side."

"Don't be ridiculous!" Megan cried. *What was wrong with these people?* "You can't desert me now! Especially to run off after some bare . . . possibility!"

Leif shrugged. "You're the one who showed us the fake gem. I think it needs to be followed up."

"All right, then—if that's how you feel, the Graf here or Colonel Vojak can pick somebody dependable to go to Vienna."

Some nonrole-playing character, she thought. *Or maybe—*

"How about Sergei Chernevsky? We know he's loyal."

"You'd cheat him out of his chance to be a Hussar?" David asked with mock horror. "For shame!"

"Look," Megan snapped. "I think this Vienna thing is just a wild-goose chase. The real action is here in Latvinia!"

She tried appealing to Leif. "You threw the fact that I'm not the real princess in my face. But what about her? We still have a rescue to stage."

"So far, we haven't gotten much closer to that," Leif pointed out. He turned to von Esbach. "You and Colonel Vojak have had people out searching for some sign of Princess Gwenda. How much longer will it take to sweep the area of Grauheim?"

Von Esbach spread his hands. "It is very wild, desolate country—"

"What would you say? A week? Ten days?"

The prime minister nodded unhappily. "It could take as long as that." He pulled out his pocket watch and consulted it. "The afternoon train for Vienna departs in an hour and a half. Otherwise you must put off your journey until tomorrow."

Megan rounded on him. "You, too?"

"Their minds are made up, Your Majesty," Esbach replied gently. "I will have a closed carriage—without the royal coat of arms—ready for you within the hour. Do you gentlemen need help in packing?

"No," Leif replied. "I always keep a small portmanteau ready."

Sure, Megan thought. *Given the Baron von Hengist's slightly shady past, he'd always have a bag ready to skip out on hotels or make other hasty departures.*

"I, too, am prepared to travel light," David spoke up.

"Do you wish to accompany them, ma'am?" von Esbach asked Megan.

"Yes," she replied, "preferably without a brass band. Let's try to be inconspicuous."

I'll still have the ride to the station to try to change their minds, Megan thought, hiding a frown.

Even though the carriage was large, it was fairly crowded inside. Besides Megan, Leif, and David, P.J. had insisted on coming along. And then there was the beefy young soldier in the ill-fitting suit—the bodyguard that von Esbach insisted should accompany her. "The assistant coachman will also accompany you on the station platform," the prime minister told her.

Megan's fingers twitched the long skirt of the black riding costume she wore. So much for inconspicuous. They'd still be a parade, even if the brass band was missing.

Whether it was the cramped quarters, the extra witness, or just her own annoyance, Megan's attempts at persuading the boys to stay crashed and burned miserably.

David and Leif would barely discuss their decision, or any plans they might have on their fictitious trip. The more they evaded her attempts to talk, the more a nagging suspicion grew in her mind.

These guys know something they're not telling me, Megan thought.

But she wasn't going to get it out of them here and now, standing on the platform of the Herzen train station. There were two trains on the tracks, pointed in opposite directions. One had boxcars, several coaches, and a crowd bustling around it. That was the Vienna Limited. The other was a single coach with a locomotive.

Megan turned to her bodyguard, indicating the quieter train. "Where is that going?"

He replied with a shrug of his heavy shoulders. "Your Majesty, I do not know. It is someone's private train."

The equivalent of a personal jet, Megan thought, now noticing that the single car on the private train looked considerably more impressive than even the first-class coach on the Vienna Limited. Heavy velvet curtains hung in the windows, cutting off the view of an undoubtedly opulent interior.

I wonder if we royals have a train of our own? Megan wondered. Then she realized she'd probably seen it— the derailed wreck from which the real Princess Gwenda had been kidnapped.

With a little shudder, she gripped Leif and David's hands. "Be careful," she told them. A second later she felt like a fool. They weren't traveling to far-off Vienna, after all. Most likely, they'd be synching out of Latvinia as soon as the train was out of the station.

"You fellas bring us something purty from Vienna," P.J. said with a grin, shaking hands with David and Leif. Both boys bowed and kissed Megan's hand, which only made her feel more conspicuous. They boarded the Vienna Limited, to appear a moment later in the one of the windows of the first-class coach. Steam wafted along the platform as the locomotive began chuffing, getting ready to leave. The conductor cried out the Latvinian equivalent of "All aboard!" The bustle around them intensified.

Megan raised a hand to wave at the smiling faces in the window, a strange feeling in her heart. They'd told her that they'd be gone for only a week, but this felt like a permanent goodbye.

Then the train lurched into motion. P.J., ever the boisterous cowboy, ran along the platform, keeping beside the first-class carriage, waving. Megan crushed the lacy little handkerchief she'd intended to flutter in her hand.

She couldn't tell if it came from the program or from the recesses of her own brain. But she had the strangest premonition that she'd never see her friends in Latvinia again.

Aboard the train, Leif waved his farewell to Princess Megan, then laughingly waved to P.J. until the train finally outpaced him. He turned to David, who was laughing and waving as well.

David's expression became a little more serious as they sat down on plushly upholstered seats. But he still had the look of a little kid who's unexpectedly gotten out of school.

"I wonder," David said mischievously. "What do you

think would happen if I came back here as a proxy and began preaching socialist revolution?"

"Going by Roberta's track record, I expect you'd probably get run over by a garbage truck in the real world." Leif retorted. "I don't know if Latvinia is bad news, but it sure as heck feels like bad luck."

"Speaking of which," David glanced around the train carriage. "When do we blow this candy stand?"

Leif frowned. He'd sort of been wondering the same thing, himself. "I suppose we ought to stick around until we reach the border . . . just in case this turns out to be some sort of a plot development."

He opened his traveling bag, slipping his hand inside to touch the purchase he'd made, sneaking down into Herzen before his departure. The butt of the automatic pistol felt nothing at all like the hilt of his sword. But Leif was taking no chances on being caught unarmed on this adventure.

Oblivious, David peered out the window as the city-scape turned into countryside. "We're making more speed on the rails than we could have in the car on the local roads," he said. "Not much farther to the border."

He grinned. "So, exactly how do you intend to spend your newfound free time?"

Leif shrugged. "I'm sure I'll find something interesting to do."

They jacked out right after the train passed through the border customs station. Leif blinked to find himself lying in brilliant afternoon sun. It had been cloudy in Latvinia—an appropriate background for their goodbyes. Rubbing his face, he got off the computer-link couch and began wandering around the empty apartment.

What *was* he going to do with his newfound free

time? He'd missed lunch with all the excitement over
Roberta Hendry, but when he stepped into the kitchen,
he discovered he wasn't really hungry. Warming up the
holo in the living room, he flicked through several talk
shows, a holosoap, and finally landed on an animated
show he'd been meaning to check out. It was about an
aging costumed crimefighter, the third generation in the
business, who wants to pass along the torch—and the
cowl—to his son. But the young man wants nothing to
do with chasing criminals.

The old man was definitely not pleased. His face
seemed to lean out of the holo display, shouting. "You
think crime will just disappear if you turn your back on
it? Not in this city. So what are you going to do? Go
away? Leave other people to deal with the problems?
Run away with your tail between your legs?"

With a sharp order Leif cut the broadcast. This was
not what he wanted to be hearing right now. He slumped
back on the living room couch, staring up at the ceiling.

This is ridiculous, he thought. *Sitting in front of the
holo with nothing on. Maybe I should take up stamp
collecting. . . .*

Abruptly Leif sat up straight. He'd thought of something to do—clearing out some of the folders in his virtmail system. Besides messages going back and forth,
that was where Leif's Net robots were supposed to dump
any information they'd been programmed to pick up.

Leif had a wide range of interests, from gossip about
society friends to swimsuit models. His searchbots
would wander the Net, finding a print reference here, a
holoclip or a photo there, and deposit their finds into
folders in a variety of categories. Now Leif began going
through the files, deleting the obvious junk, filing other
items, putting some aside to be examined further.

When he reached the "Fencing" folder, he hesitated for a moment, then shook his head.

You're not in Latvinia anymore, he told himself. *The ceiling's not going to fall in because you show an interest in swords.*

Telling the computer to open the folder, Leif shifted to a more comfortable position on the couch. There were a couple of gossipy items about adversaries he'd faced on the fencing strip, an offer for bargain saber blades— Russian steel, not the best. He deleted that.

Then came a reference to a new fencing-related multimedia display. Leif always left standing orders for his searchbots to store references to fencing in historical holodramas. Hollywood swordfights were often ridiculous—they went on way too long, and usually used techniques that would never work against a real opponent. But Leif never missed a chance to check one out.

This was something different, however—a documentary titled *Fencing: From Martial Art to Sport.* Leif checked the ordering information. The price wasn't exorbitant for a specialty item. In a few moments, Leif's credit account was a slight tad lighter, and the documentary was downloading.

Leif told the computer to play his new purchase. It started with a scene of fencers bouting in a modern salle. Leif made a face. These guys weren't all that good. Then the display shifted to a flatpicture engraving of an eighteenth century fencing school—the House of Angelo in London. A narrator explained that in this period, fencing was actually dueling practice. A flurry of images appeared—people from various eras getting skewered in duels.

The documentary editors were doing their best to keep the presentation visually interesting, but Leif felt his eyes glazing over as the story moved on about a hundred years, explaining how the rise of the middle class helped push the sword from its dominant position as a gentleman's weapon. Engravings and painted portraits began giving way to photographs. Leif began fast-forwarding, stopping only when he saw a saber in someone's hand.

He let the documentary run on when it discussed the influence of Giuseppe Radelli, the father of modern saber technique. But he sent the display zooming on again, slowing it to chuckle at the herky-jerky antics of a couple of fencers captured on flatfilm by somebody named Lumiere. He zipped ahead to another famous flatfilm swordfighting movie, *The Mark of Zorro* with a very athletic actor named Douglas Fairbanks.

Leif leaned forward on the couch. Something in that set of wildly flickering images . . .

He ordered the computer cue back to the earlier film, and then to proceed—slowly. He was just about to give up and fast-forward again when the computer displayed a hundred-and-something-year-old photograph. It was a short, thick-bodied guy with cropped hair and a funny-looking beard. He stood posing in an old-fashioned, almost prissy guard position, flat-footed, his free hand on his hip.

Leif knew where he'd seen that pose—and that face—before. He'd squared off against that guy in the palace gardens of Latvinia!

"Computer!" he barked, ordering the display back to that picture. "Does the presentation have any hypertext information on the subject of this photograph?

"Information available," the computer replied. Leif silently blessed the scholarly heart of whoever made this documentary. "Subject is one Louis Rondelle, French military officer and fencing master—"

Listening to Louis Rondelle's military exploits fighting German invaders in 1873, his training in the use of the sword, and the training he imparted to his students, Leif's eyes grew steadily wider.

I was lucky to get off as lightly as I did, he thought ruefully. *This guy could have probably taken my head off!*

He stopped the presentation, asking the computer instead to display all portraits of fencing masters shown in the documentary from 1880 to 1900, along with any hypertext biographies.

Yes—he began to spot several other familiar faces, those tough-looking guys surrounding Gray Piotr at the Latvinian court. There was another bearded Frenchman—Georges Robert Ainé. A fierce-looking Italian Master glared over a bristling mustache—Luigi Barbasetti. Leif remembered another Frenchman, Augustin Grisin, for his brilliantined receding hair, his sharp eyes, and the wry twist of his lips.

Then there were the two fencing masters stripped to the waist and squaring off for a duel. One had craggy features, a hook of a nose, and muscles in his back, shoulders and arms like a woodcutter. That was Athos de San Malato. His opponent, smaller with a rounder face, curly hair, and a mustache, was Eugenio Pini.

Leif even found the face of the assassin who'd almost killed him—who was, of course, renowned for his mastery of the centuries-old art of fighting with rapier and dagger.

"Holy cow!" Leif muttered. "No wonder I got my ass handed to me in Latvinia. Alan Slaney has surrounded himself with the Murderers' Row of fencing!"

13

P.J. Farris chuckled, ending his mad dash down the platform of the Herzen station, still waving to the departing Vienna Limited. To his left, the waiting locomotive gave a great *chuff!* of steam and began to move.

And behind him he heard a brief, surprised female cry.

That was Megan's voice!

P.J. whirled around. Both Megan's coachman and her bodyguard were down on the platform, while a quartet of well-dressed men dragged a squirming, cloak-wrapped figure toward the moving private train.

"The princess!" P.J. cried. "They're abducting the princess!"

Most of the crowd on the platform was either unaware of the scuffle, or prudently avoiding it. Now people began to turn. One of the struggling abductors—the one who'd donated his cloak for wrapping Megan—threw away the club he'd used to take out her protectors. His hand darted into his frock coat, coming out with a shiny automatic pistol.

Two shots into the air, and the area around the kidnappers was magically cleared.

P.J. caught a glimpse of red and scarlet at the platform entrance as he fought a surge of panicked onlookers. "Guardsmen!" he called. "Kidnappers! They're taking the princess!"

The young Texan finally fought free of the crowd as the kidnappers unceremoniously bundled Megan onto the parlor car. Then they began leaping in themselves. P.J. loped along the now-empty platform, tearing open his long coat. Underneath, a bright red sash was wrapped round his waist—and the butt of one of his Army Colts stuck out from where the gun was tucked into the sash.

But where was his target? The abductors were now aboard. Gun in hand, P.J. ran to try and catch up with the departing parlor car.

From the front of the train, the engineer leaned out of the locomotive, aiming a pistol. P.J. snapped a shot. The trainman's gun clattered to the platform as he clapped both hands to his face, lurching backwards. P.J. thought he'd taken the man out, but the train suddenly shot forward, moving at a speed that had to threaten the old Civil War-era locomotive's boiler.

"Mr. Texas!" a semifamiliar voice cried. P.J. turned to see Sergei Chernevsky running toward him. The young hussar's half-cape streamed in the wind. He held a saber in one hand, a horse pistol in the other. More soldiers clustered around the downed bodyguards.

"The prime minister had us stationed outside in case

of trouble," Chernevsky said. "This is far worse than we imagined."

"They're escaping!" P.J. interrupted. "We need horses!"

They headed outside to the street, where the cavalry mounts were tied up. But Sergei didn't seem very hopeful. "That's the spur line to the mines on Mount Doom," he said, pointing to a craggy peak in the distance. "The tracks go back and forth—"

"Switchbacks," P.J. said.

"And trains must slow down for them," Sergei finished. "But the trainman—when you shot him, he fell across the locomotive's throttle—it will not slow!"

P.J. was already untying the reins of the two fastest-looking horses. "Then climb aboard!" he said, swinging into the saddle. "We've got a runaway train to catch!"

Megan O'Malley didn't get to see much of her abduction. One moment she'd been waving goodbye, the next—darkness surrounded her as the cloak was thrown over her. She'd been wrapped up like a mummy, but to judge from the quiet groans on either side of her, both bodyguards had been taken out.

She got to *feel* what happened next—three, maybe four sets of strong hands manhandling her along while she tried to wriggle free of the enclosing woolen folds.

Megan heard P.J. yell, and then a couple of gunshots. Then she was unceremoniously heaved into the air to land with a thump on a metal floor.

The other train, she thought. *They're making their getaway on the other train!*

The clatter of feet around her told Megan that her abductors were boarding as well. Then she was half-dragged, half-rolled through a doorway and onto a carpeted floor.

We must be inside the parlor car, she thought.

Her bundled form was heaved up again, then dumped onto something that felt like a cross between a bench and a settee.

Megan immediately set to work trying to get free of the heavy cloak that enwrapped her. She managed to get her head free of the stifling folds, losing her hat and veil in the process. The inside of the railroad car looked like one of the more opulent sitting rooms in the palace. Patterned red silk covered the walls, broken by purple velvet drapes at the windows. Costly oriental carpets were spread across the floors. Several large armchairs were scattered about, besides the bench-style settee by the door where she'd been dumped. A large mahogany table dominated the center of the room, with two hurricane lamps to give light. The faceted crystal ornaments dangling from the lamps tinkled together as the train began to pick up speed and sent little refracted rainbows of light scattering through the car.

Three of her abductors stood by the table, where the apparent leader was shouting into a speaking tube. "We're aboard, Zoltan. What? Running after? Well, shoot him, you fool!"

The fourth kidnapper loomed over her, looking like the villain in an old-time play in his black suit and tall hat. He was even twirling his long, black, waxed mustache.

"Now, my pretty—" the kidnapper began.

While he'd been preening, Megan had continued to work at getting free. Now she had one arm loose. She made a fist—and rammed it full-force into an area where no male likes to be punched.

"*OOOOOWWWWWWWWWWWWWUUUGGGGGH!*"
The kidnapper made a horrible noise, folding at the middle. He completely forgot about his mustache, clutching at a more personal part of his anatomy.

Megan was almost free of the cape, now. Her hand shot forward, snatching the hilt of the sword at the kidnapper's waist as he sank to the carpeted floor. Rising up as he went down, she unsheathed a splendid straight-bladed saber. A Wilkinson British cavalry saber—a pair were displayed on the wall of the virtual training room in Alan's salle.

The trio around the table turned to her as she kicked the cape away and stepped around her incapacitated captor, who was now groaning and pounding the floor.

Now the nearest of the three—big, blond, and clean-shaven—stepped forward, his hand on the hilt of his own sword. "Don't be foolish, Princess," he began. "It's three against one—"

But he was the foolish one, advancing into attack range with only a foot of his blade showing out of the scabbard. Megan lunged forward, her blade slicing into the muscles of his thigh.

Blondie collapsed with a surprisingly high-pitched cry, trying desperately to stop the flow of blood.

The remaining two had to get past the big mahogany table to come at her. They came round on opposite sides, swords drawn and ready.

To Megan's left was a short, wiry guy with dark, intense features. She'd seen him around the salle sometimes, with Alan and the more advanced saber students. On the right was a beefy, red-haired guy with a huge handlebar mustache. He held his sword in his left hand and looked as if he knew how to use it.

"Frack this chivalry stuff," Big Red growled, coming

forward as the train lurched into greater speed. He brought his sword up and around in a swooping cut.

It was a frankly murderous blow that would have split Megan's head like a melon—if it had landed. But the left-handed swordsman's wide swing tangled his blade in the velvet drapes. And as he tried to pull free, Megan moved in a reverse lunge, stepping back to gain the room to thrust straight at Big Red's shoulder.

Her saber pierced flesh and then grated into bone. Megan realized that her point was actually in the joint. She twisted, popping the shoulder the way she'd disjointed the legs on last Thanksgiving's turkey.

That realization made her a little queasy as she faced the final kidnapper. Maybe it made her careless, as well. She never saw the guy she'd sucker-punched until he was right behind her, going for a tackle to sweep her feet out from under her.

Megan made an undignified landing, right on her butt. She managed to kick the sneak attacker right in the face.

But the last swordsman was looming over her, his sword upraised. . . .

P.J. Farris rode crouched over his cavalry mount, urging the animal to greater speed as they galloped along the track right of way with Sergei close behind. They quickly passed through Herzen's tiny manufacturing district and then were out of town. The train was well ahead, screeching through a mild curve in the tracks.

If they hit anything sharper at that speed, they'll definitely derail, P.J. thought unhappily. *Unless the boiler blows up first.*

In the distance he saw a knot of people standing by the tracks, some mounted, others holding extra horses.

Sergei saw them, too. "That is the real getaway," he

declared. "The train was to get out of town. Then they'd ride cross-country."

But the planned rendezvous wasn't kept. Despite wavings and shoutings up ahead, the locomotive thundered past. A couple of the waiting conspirators tried to spur after the parlor car. But when the rest spotted Sergei's uniform, they scrambled into the saddle and began tearing out of there.

"We're never going to beat that thing in a straight chase," P.J. called, watching the train outrun the pursuing riders. "Is there some way to cut across the way it's going?"

Sergei pointed up ahead. "There's a path that goes up the lower slope, but it's very steep—better for mountain goats than horses."

"We'll have to try it," P.J. replied. *And take the chance,* he thought.

Sergei's path was even worse than advertised, a bare scratch up a steep, stony slope. At points P.J.'s mount was just about jumping from rock to rock. The horse wasn't happy, especially since its rider kept urging it to greater speed. P.J. wasn't exactly delighted himself. One wrong move, and the horse would go down, probably breaking a leg. And that would mean shooting the poor animal, something he hated to do, even in a sim.

Considering how I'd look after the horse fell on me, I would probably need to be shot, too, P.J. thought. *Provided I didn't break my neck first and save everybody the trouble.*

The horse scrambled up onto the railroad tracks just after the train passed. P.J. hauled round on the reins and spurred his mount in pursuit. It was hard use for an animal, even a virtual one. The horse was blowing hard, its flanks lathered.

But P.J. didn't have a choice—not if he was going to catch up with that train.

You know it can be done, he told himself as he galloped after the back end of the parlor car. *Train robbers did it in the old days. Stunt men have been doing it for train robbery movies ever since.*

He brought his horse level with the open platform at the rear, leaning out to grab hold of the steel ladder that led to the roof of the car. P.J. missed on his first grab. Urging his steed to one final effort, he matched speeds with the train, leaned out, and caught on. Kicking loose from the stirrups, he swung from the back of the horse, his hands cramping from their desperate grip on the steel rungs. . . .

Megan scooted herself backward along the floor, frantically parrying the hammer-blows her opponent rained down on her.

Tac-tac-tac-TAC! Somehow she managed to keep her blade in the way of each of his chopping attacks. He leaned back for another swing and was thrown off balance as the train lurched, screeching through a turn. Megan took advantage of the distraction, throwing herself under the mahogany table, scrambling across the width of it, finally managing to get to her feet.

Meanwhile, on the other side, the red-haired guy she'd nailed in the shoulder pulled himself upright, tearing the curtains away from one window as he did so. He stared outside, then turned with a shout. "The backup party— the getaway horses—we just went right by them!"

Staggering, he snatched up the end of the speaking tube and blew. "Zoltan!" he yelled into the metal cup. *"ZOLTAN!"*

Then he dropped the end of the speaking tube. His

normally ruddy face, pale already, went paler still. "No answer," he announced. "We're on a runaway train!"

The blond guy with the leg wound began hopping for the rear exit. "Heck with this!" he yelled. "I'm getting out of here!"

He jumped, but his scream as he landed cut through the noise of the chugging of the locomotive like a horrible parody of a train whistle. The red-headed guy looking out the window shuddered.

Megan took a deep breath. The only other way out of this mess was to go through the front of the car, across the coal tender, and into the locomotive. And she—and her sword—were in the way.

The last armed kidnapper came at her with fury in his eyes. His blade beat against Megan's as he tried to get past her guard with sheer physical force. Each time she managed to get her saber back in line—but she was being forced to retreat along the side of the big table. Once he had more room to get at her . . .

Finally he managed to pin her weapon against the mahogany tabletop. His eyes burned as he reached for the wrist of her sword arm.

And then P.J. Farris was advancing through the car, his big Colt leveled.

The dark-haired swordsman's yell was more a scream of frustration. He brought his saber back—was P.J. too late?

14

Megan twisted desperately, trying to get free of the iron grip on her wrist holding her implacably in place for the final, fatal, slash.

P.J.'s big Army Colt boomed in the tight confines of the parlor car.

The dark-haired kidnapper was probably dead even before he hit the floor.

Even as he fell, however, the swordsman wasn't through. His blade whistled through the air as he twisted from the bullet's impact. The Wilkinson saber in his hand shattered one of the crystal lamps on the table. Oil spattered onto the carpet and the drapes. The furnishings in the wooden train car might be opulent, but they weren't fireproof. Flames immediately began licking along the rich fabrics.

"Over here!" Megan called desperately to P.J.

He made it to her side of the parlor car just before the spreading fire cut them off. The two remaining kidnappers, slowed by injury, remained screaming on the other side.

Megan and P.J. burst onto the forward platform to face a big bin full of coal—the tender. Over the chugging of the laboring locomotive, they could hear an ominous hiss. "That boiler's going to go!" P.J. panted.

Great, Megan thought. *A choice between being blown up or roasted to death. The things I do for fun!* She pointed between the two cars. "The coupling!" she shouted.

P.J. leaned down, trying to disconnect their car from the train. He even kicked desperately at the coupling. "Need a lever," he said.

Megan looked at the Wilkinson saber in her hand—thirty-four inches of the world's finest steel. Wordlessly, she handed the sword to P.J. He jammed it into the stuck coupling, heaving with all his strength.

It was an ignoble end for the sword, which broke. But so did the coupling. The locomotive shot forward. The parlor car rolled on a bit from sheer inertia. Then gravity started pulling it back along the rails.

"Gotta jump before it picks up too much speed the other way!" P.J. shouted. He made a cowboy's idea of a courtly gesture. "After you, ma'am!"

Gathering her long skirts together, Megan jumped. She hit the ground hard, rolling along the gravel-bedded railroad tracks.

Between my butt and my shoulders, I'm going to have some glorious bruises tomorrow, she thought. *What next? Splinters from the wooden railroad ties?*

From up ahead came an earth-shaking roar like the end of the world. The locomotive's boiler had blown up! Megan was suddenly glad she was already hugging the ground.

P.J.'s voice sounded slightly tinny in her ears as he slowly pushed himself up. "Come on, your Majesty, we've got a long walk back to town. Sergei was ridin' along after me, so he should be able to help. . . ."

He looked back along the tracks, toward the still-moving parlor car. By now, even the roof was ablaze.

"Providin', of course, that the Rolling Inferno there doesn't run him over first."

P.J. extended his hand. Slowly, shakily, Megan got herself to her feet. They began hiking along the tracks, back in the direction of Herzen.

After only a few minutes, Megan was painfully aware that she wasn't wearing walking shoes. She glanced over at P.J., who was also limping slightly.

"Not as bad as high-stacked cowboy boots," he said, ruefully holding out a pair of finely made city shoes. "But not designed for a stroll like this, either."

At that moment, they heard approaching hoofbeats. P.J. looked up. "Good old Sergei."

The arrival of Sergei Chernevsky solved Megan's traveling problems. The gallant young Hussar insisted that she ride his horse. It wasn't the most comfortable seat, considering where some of Megan's bruises were located. Also, her voluminous skirts required that she ride side-saddle—women didn't sit astride horses in this era, after all, especially not princesses. At least the cavalry mount wasn't feeling frisky. It was too exhausted after a long, uphill chase.

The boys weren't moving too quickly either. By the time a cavalry contingent met them, drawn by the locomotive explosion, both P.J. and Sergei looked pretty footsore.

The lieutenant in charge of the search party immediately dispatched a messenger back to the Graf von Esbach. The prime minister arrived with a carriage almost as soon as they reached level ground again. Megan piled pillows around herself and leaned back, closing her eyes. She could smell smoke coming off her clothes, and was sure that she looked a sight.

A very long, very hot bath, she promised herself.

Then she remembered this was veeyar. All she really had to do was cut her connection.

Von Esbach's quiet voice cut into her thoughts. "Did Your Majesty recognize any of the men who abducted you?"

Megan opened her eyes. "No, but I could describe them."

As she ran through detailed descriptions of the quartet of kidnappers, the prime minister shook his head. "None of them sound like members of Gray Piotr's inner circle. Of course, he could have hired some desperate men to do the job—"

"They were dressed like gentlemen," Megan said, "even if they acted like villains from an old melodrama. At least two of them knew how to handle a sword."

"The redheaded one—he sounds like the person who approached me in the other plot I mentioned," Sergei said.

The jealous AHSO members, Megan remembered. *Just wonderful. I've got at least two sets of enemies, and half the people I can trust have pulled out on me.*

The adrenalin high that had pushed through this whole little adventure was finally wearing off. Megan hid a sudden yawn. She also tried to stretch, groaning at the response from her stiffening muscles.

This princess business isn't all it's cracked up to be, she thought.

All of a sudden she was looking forward to reality and tomorrow's simple, prosaic fencing lesson.

In his family's Washington apartment, Leif Anderson sat on the living room couch, frowning at the images on the holographic display. With his computer's help, he'd edited the multimedia presentation on fencing, culling all the references to the various masters he now recognized into one file. It was pretty amazing.

At a sudden thought he checked the copyright date on the presentation. The thing had just come out. There was no way Alan Slaney could have cribbed his inner circle from this presentation. That meant he must have been mining fencing history, assembling the necessary research to create those fencing masters as characters, for—how long?

Leif went back over his confrontation with Louis Rondelle. The short, tough Frenchman had seemed like a real person, not a nonrole-playing character responding to a program. If Rondelle was a typical creation, Latvinia began to look less like a labor of love and more like the product of obsession.

Well, well, well, Leif thought. *Mr. Alan "Aw, Shucks" Slaney has some hidden depths.*

Leif headed into the kitchen. One good thing about this particular distraction. His stomach had quieted down, and he was ready to eat something. He constructed a sandwich and stood at the kitchen counter, frowning as he chewed.

When you come down to it, he suddenly thought, *what do we really know about Alan Slaney?*

Everybody (including Leif) had simply hung a "nice guy" label on Slaney and left it at that.

From what I've heard about Slaney, he comes off as trustworthy, loyal, helpful, friendly, courteous, kind, obedient, cheerful, thrifty, brave, clean, and reverent— all the old Boy Scout virtues. Well, maybe that's not surprising. They came into being in the early 1900s, after the Boer War.

In fact, Alan embodied many of the qualities of the heroes from the novels Latvinia was set up to emulate. He was honorable, pleasant, hardworking, good at sport—and fencing, a gentleman's sport, at that.

On the other hand, no gentleman of Ruritanian romance would dream of making a living as a glorified janitor, Leif thought. *I guess you could add "modest" to the developing character profile.*

Add it all up, and a cynical voice at the back of Leif's head whispered, "Too good to be true."

Leif finished his sandwich, cleaned the dishes, and headed down the hallway to his room. What he intended to do now might require tools that he wasn't about to leave traces of on the family's home system.

He checked over the computer-link couch, sat back, closed his eyes, and linked in. This time he went to his virtual workspace, the Icelandic stave house of his dreams. Leif opened his eyes sitting on the living room couch and immediately headed for the floor-to-ceiling shelves set against one wall. Literally thousands of tiny 3-D icons, each representing a different program, stood ranked in front of him.

Pursing his lips, Leif began choosing his weapons: a glowing question mark; an icon like a fiery red shovel; and finally a bone-white skeleton holding a stylized key. Something told him that if he wanted the true story on

Alan Slaney, he'd need something more than the usual search engines.

Holding up each icon separately in the palm of his hand, he imparted specific instructions. As he did, each of the little doodads flashed and disappeared.

Okay, they're off and searching the Net at the speed of light, Leif thought. *But that doesn't mean they'll be back with anything very fast. What do I do in the mean-time?*

Of course, there were still all those virtmail folders to go through.

Leif did not do a great job of sorting, half-distracted as he was. Several items he'd probably end up wanting were instead carelessly trashed. But it helped pass the time while his specialized Net agents did a quick once-over of Alan Slaney's past and present life.

The question-mark program was the most general-purpose of the three, making all the usual general in-quiries—date of birth, upbringing, schooling, etc. Its most off-beat quality was that it was more persistent and less selective than most search engines, harvesting a wide field of data.

The red shovel was more specialized; in fact, it was very selective. It looked specifically for dirt on a given subject—brushes with the law, arrests, police records, criminal and civil court cases, stuff like that. Unless a judicial seal had been placed on the records, that pro-gram could usually worm information out of any public databases.

The skeleton key program went even farther, checking for dirt in private files that normally weren't available to the general public—or most entry-grade hackers.

When he got the signal that the low-order profile had

been compiled, Leif cheerfully stopped messing around with his folders and began reading.

Nothing really seemed to leap out at Leif. Alan Slaney was indeed as old as he said he was. He grew up in New York City, the only son of a nice middle-class family. His grades weren't just good, they were spectacular. Young Alan was quite the whiz kid. His parents began moving around the country, finding schools that would promote their son to classes matching his ability. Alan finally wound up graduating from college at a time most kids were trying to decide which high school they would attend.

But college represented the first big check for young Alan—he tried out for the fencing team there, but was repeatedly beaten by larger, older, and more experienced opponents. Could that be why he turned to the more scholarly approach of historical fencing? Leif wondered.

Not satisfied with a bachelor's degree in political science, Alan went on to win a doctorate in record time.

Then . . . a blank. No jobs, no schooling—

Leif blinked. Wait a minute. That wasn't exactly a surprise. Alan would have been only about seventeen. He wouldn't be going to school anymore, and what sort of job would a seventeen-year-old expect to win? Most kids would be slinging hamburgers or ice cream at that age.

The next hit came from legal records—a will from Alan's parents being probated. Leif dug back. That looked okay—a car accident. Alan wound up with a house and a little money. A couple of years later there he was selling the house, moving to Washington, and setting himself up.

Not exactly a surprise for a job-seeking poli sci wonk

to come to the nation's capital. If you want to play politics, this was the biggest arena available.

But it didn't explain how an apparent genius with a background in political science wound up as little more than a maintenance man.

Alan hadn't killed anybody, at least according to police records. In fact, he hadn't even been caught spitting on the sidewalk. So why wasn't he working in his field? Politicians always needed aides—the brighter, the better. Somebody had to write speeches, do the research on bills and issues, not to mention all the grunt-work involved in getting someone elected, installed, and working in high office.

Through his father, Leif knew of several likable pols who were probably more cunning than smart—kept afloat by the staff people they'd assembled around them.

Why would a supposedly nice guy like Alan Slaney not fit in? Leif called up his searchbots and gave orders for them to search harder. Ah. Here were mentions of a couple of internships—which quickly went nowhere.

Was Alan the lone-genius type, not able to fit in with a team? The guys he'd briefly worked for were pretty much on opposing ends of the political spectrum.

What were Alan's own political views?

Maybe the easiest way to find out was to take a look at his thesis. A quick order to the search program, and a copy of the archived thesis was immediately downloaded. Leif looked at the title: *The Fin de Siècle—A Final Opportunity Lost*.

So, Leif thought, Alan's fascination with that time period started pretty young. He began scanning through densely written pages of scholarly mumbo-jumbo.

The more he read, the wider his eyes got. Alan Slaney certainly had an . . . *interesting* point of view.

As seen by him, the *Fin de Siècle* was truly a golden age for the great Western powers. Human relations were enhanced by the traditions of social restraint.

Funny, Leif thought. Most people considered that era to be an age of prudery, hypocrisy, even oppression. If those traditions were so great, why were women out fighting so hard to get the vote?

Back to Alan . . . in international politics, self-control was also the watchword. These were the great days of the Concert of Europe, when nations could sit down and iron out differences around a conference table instead of a battlefield.

Except for Russia and Japan having that nasty little war, and America and Spain, not to mention most of the Western powers intervening in China for the Boxer Rebellion. And those were only the high points Leif remembered from history classes. A quick look at a history timeline and he tallied two more wars in the Balkans between 1912 and 1913, involving six different countries in various sides and combinations, which eventually led to World War I, as well as a number of smaller disturbances all over the globe.

But the most worrisome part of Alan's version of the turn of the century fairyland was what he called "a clearly defined social compact." Leif translated that as certain people knowing their place and staying in it.

He shook his head, suddenly reminded of how unwelcome David had been made to feel in Latvinia.

I expected to find that Slaney had a skeleton in his closet, he thought. *Instead, there seems to be a burning cross!*

For a long time Leif continued to sit in the living room of his virtual work space, trying to decide what he ought to do. What he'd discovered wasn't exactly illegal. It was very distasteful, though. Would Megan appreciate learning that her wonderful pal Alan Slaney had feet of clay—and *dirty* clay, at that?

No, Leif told himself. *If I go to Megan with this, it will just look like sour grapes on my part. She already thinks I bailed from Latvinia because I couldn't hack it there.*

On the other hand, he couldn't keep this new information to himself.

In the end he decided to discuss it with someone whose opinion he respected—someone who would be personally interested in his discoveries, as well.

David Gray looked surprised when Leif called him.

His image floated in the display of the virtual computer console in the virtual living room.

Obviously, David recognized the background from Leif's image. "I see you're in your fortress of solitude. What's up?"

"It has to do with our little walk through Herzen. I was wrong, and you were right. I've come across a couple of things about Alan Slaney, and I need to discuss them with someone who has a cool head. Can you synch in for a while? I warn you, it may take some time."

David grinned. "I think I can fit you into my busy schedule. Give me a couple of minutes."

Soon enough, he appeared in Leif's workspace. "What dark secrets have you uncovered?"

"It all started when I encountered this picture in a presentation on old-time fencing," Leif began. From the picture of Louis Rondelle, he went on to explain how he'd identified a number of other members of Gray Piotr's inner circle. "All this seemed like a surprise—"

"Coming from Prince Charming," David finished. "Knowing you, I expect you've already gotten the low-down on our oh-so-nice friend."

"I've barely scratched the surface," Leif said, "but already I've turned up some stuff I don't like very much." He explained about Alan's accelerated academic career. "You've got to read his doctoral thesis to believe it," he ended.

David looked surprised. "Why isn't he using the thesis to get a job?"

"I think you'll be more interested in the content of his paper than Alan's employment or lack thereof," Leif said. "It explains a lot about his sim. You should read it."

"Okay," David said, his face showing no expression. "Maybe I should."

Leif sat and fidgeted while David went through the holotext version of the downloaded manuscript. The process took even longer than he'd expected. Where Leif had only skimmed, David was actually wading through large sections of Alan Slaney's scholarly prose.

It took all of Leif's patience not to start reading over his friend's shoulder, pointing out what he considered to be the relevant parts of the thesis.

Finally David turned away from the glittering text display. "Very . . . interesting," he said.

"Interesting?" Leif echoed. "I think *appalling* is the more appropriate description. How can you, of all people, be so calm after reading what that—that jerk had to say?"

"Well, he's not just a racist," David replied. "I'd say he was more of an equal-opportunity reactionary. He's not a fascist, either. I expect the proper label would be to call him a classical conservative."

"What's the difference?" Leif wanted to know.

"Alan's kind of conservatism is the nineteenth-century kind—the sort that wanted to keep things as they were back then in the old days. World politics was a sort of 'rich white guys who picked their parents well' club." David's smile turned wry. "To those guys, today's so-called conservatives would seem like rabble-rousing radicals—"

"But that's what they are," Leif said.

David continued as if he hadn't been interrupted. "Who are in favor of way too much democracy."

Leif closed his mouth with a snap.

David gestured back to the displayed text. "Once you get past his sugar-coated view of the *Fin de Siècle*, Slaney actually has a logical argument. He suggests that the turn of the century was the last chance for what he calls 'the better classes' to stem the currents that pushed Europe into World War I."

Leif frowned. "More like 'keep the lid on,' I think. Things were happening all over—France, Britain, the Balkans, the Far East, Russia, and Africa."

David nodded. "The tide had been running against Alan's heroes for a good fifty years. Art and science and many men of letters were, for the most part, on the enemy side. When you've got people as diverse as George Bernard Shaw and Sigmund Freud saying that the status quo was no good, you've got problems."

Leif's friend spread his hands in an all-inclusive gesture. "That's why I say Alan's an equal-opportunity reactionary. He's not just about people of color keeping in their place, but about everybody staying in their place: working folks, union types, artists, what we'd consider the lower middle class, women, you name it."

His tone grew a bit more pointed at Leif's shrug. "For instance, he probably wouldn't be too wild about someone like your father making a fortune. That, too, would be rocking the traditional boat."

"The guy's a nut!" Leif burst out.

"He just has a very different point of view," David responded. "I might not like it, but I think I can understand it. In the history of the world according to Slaney, the methods used to vent off the steam gathering among the diverse people threatening the traditional systems—national pride, imperialism—that's what brought on World War I. And what came out of World War I is what has led to the world today."

"I don't think we came out so badly," Leif said.

"But we have lost some things from that earlier

world," David argued. "Today, things like individualism, privacy—they're in short supply. Personal honor isn't as widespread or as trustworthy. Causes were considered to be bigger than people then—that later bred political expediency. Mass politics, mass economics—wouldn't you like to be thought of as something more than a faceless consumer? Even information has become a commodity."

"You might have a point. But Slaney's alternative would be to turn the clock back about a hundred and twenty years. Can you imagine what that would mean?"

David gave a curt nod. "Not all that much honor to be found in a cotton field," he said. "But it would have been nice for all of us to pick up some of those old ideals along the way."

"In theory," Leif said.

"In theory," David agreed with a sigh. "But out in the practical world, the classical conservatives made some pretty bad choices. For instance, in Germany, they backed Adolf Hitler, figuring they could use him to stop the slide."

"And we all know how that turned out," Leif said. "So I was right. Slaney *is* a fascist."

"He's a romantic," David corrected, "holding to a set of beliefs that just don't fit in the world we live in."

"Maybe that's why he came up with Latvinia," Leif suggested. "He created an environment friendly to his point of view"—he gestured from himself to David—"and unfriendly to others."

"Makes sense," David admitted. Then he frowned. "But I think we're missing something, somewhere."

"That helps narrow things down," Leif said sarcastically.

"If I knew what it was that we're missing, we wouldn't have to look for it," David responded. "I propose a division of labor. You're already deep into Slaney's background—with one surprising exception."

Leif blinked. "What?"

"His fencing," David replied. "Slaney's teaching at the salle probably takes more effort than his day job. Why don't you look into that? I'll take his other bigtime investment—Latvinia. We still don't know why he made up his own country. Maybe we can learn a few things from *how* he went about building it."

David synched out from Leif's stave house and transited to his own virtual workspace. This month, he was trying out a new simulation—the bridge of one of the new deep-space probes.

He opened his eyes to find himself in the captain's acceleration couch, facing the main control arrays.

Leif's dubious words still rang in his ears. "You act as though you can retrace Slaney's course through the Net. Unless you've been holding out on old Uncle Leif, I don't know of any software that can crack Net anonymity—or track what sites someone visited months ago."

Leif was completely right, of course. But there were other ways to peel that particular onion.

David began issuing orders to his system. When you want to build your own large-scale sim, he thought, all roads lead to the Creators' Quorum.

After all, he had some experience at shaping veeyar to his own designs. David's recreations of early spacecraft had a certain reputation among a select group of hobbyists.

And the chat room where he picked up his best simulation hints was the Creators' Quorum. Some of the biggest names in the business synched in to shoot the virtual breeze. Even Chris Rodrigues—the infamous Rod of Sarxos—turned up occasionally, it was rumored.

But nobody was sure. Lots of the visitors to the Creators' Quorum did so behind proxies. Would Alan Slaney have done that? Maybe, if he thought he had something to hide.

But as David's search agents began working their way back through discussions stretching over the past few months, he was looking for certain connections among the questions.

His profile called for intelligence, perseverance, and an interest in getting beyond the store-bought software most people used to craft the virtual realities of their choice.

"Oh, yeah," David breathed as parts of the holotext transcripts began switching over to highlighted mode. These were possible hits. His search agents also color-coded the selected portions depending on how many of the profile parameters matched.

David scowled. Even when he scanned the sections highlighted in red—the most likely possibilities—there were a lot more than he expected.

Sighing, he began to read. And read. But as he plowed through the vast amount of material, certain patterns began to emerge. The questions were numerous, posed under a variety of Net handles. But David saw a quiet agenda that tied them all together.

One set of questions, spread over a couple of months, really jumped out at him. Supposedly coming from several different participants, they essentially asked for the best methods to erase inactive computer archives to create sufficient cyberspace for a large-scale sim.

And what was Alan Slaney's daytime line of work? He maintained a building full of corporate computer systems—including tetrabytes of inactive computer archives!

Well, I've probably learned where the Latvinia sim is located—if I wanted to plow through a building's worth of memory, David thought.

He was about to dive back into that mass of holotext when he suddenly had another thought.

Beyond the other stuff we've discovered, what I've just learned is that no matter how much of a nice guy he seems to be, Alan Slaney is no angel.

16

Megan found herself back in the burning parlor car. She called to P.J. to come and join her, but this time things didn't turn out so well. As P.J. darted forward, he was surrounded in sudden sheets of flame.

"P.J.!" Megan screamed in horror.

He came staggering out of the flames, his clothes already ablaze. Megan could smell the terrible stench of burning skin.

Megan tried to beat out P.J.'s flaming clothes, but she was hampered by the way he clung to her. Then dancing flames appeared on her own heavy wool skirt. She wanted to drop and roll, just as she'd been taught in school, she wanted to get out of there, but she couldn't. P.J.'s grip had turned into an unbreakable stranglehold. The flames were a roaring inferno now, roasting her alive, and she couldn't get free—

Megan awoke to find herself struggling against her own pillow. She lay very still for a moment, letting her racing heart calm down a little.

A nightmare, she thought. *My stupid brain processing what happened in the sim and editing it into a more scary version!*

She took a deep breath, exhaling it as a long sigh. Yesterday's adventures in Latvinia had really put her through the wringer. Although she hadn't suffered in real life any of the bruises and scrapes she'd picked up in veeyar, Megan had been dog-tired when she synched out. She hadn't had anything to eat. Her energy had lasted just long enough for her to get out of her clothes and get into her bed.

One quick look at her alarm clock, and Megan groaned. She was up ridiculously early even for her early-rising household. Stretching, she padded down the hall to the bathroom to take care of some business followed by a shower to get rid of the film of cold sweat left over from her nightmare.

She was still yawning and feeling unpleasantly out of it when she emerged from the bathroom wrapped in a terrycloth robe. Maybe some food . . .

Standing in the kitchen doorway, she scanned the room in dismay. Obviously her brothers had ravaged through here last night, searching for snacks. The package of English muffins she'd hidden in the cupboard behind a row of soup cans lay empty on the kitchen counter. To add insult to injury, the boys had left the cans out for her to tidy up. Even though she loved her brothers dearly, they made her understand why the phrase "Oh, brother" had come to be used as a universal and everyday curse.

Megan went to the stove and began heating a kettle

of water. Well, at least Michael, Sean, Paul, and Rory didn't like tea. She found a scone she'd wrapped in plastic and foil and hidden under the potatoes, put a bag of English Breakfast tea in a cup, and filled it with hot water.

While waiting for the tea to steep, Megan unwrapped her scone, cut it in half and toasted it lightly, got out the butter, and found an untouched jar of imported marmalade. The butter melted on the hot, crumbly scone. She could hardly wait to cover it with orange preserves—manna from heaven.

Now the tea was ready. Megan spooned in some turbinado sugar, then went to the refrigerator for milk. There was only a single container there, which contained a tiny dribble of liquid, barely enough to change the color of the tea. Brothers!

Well, I'm a bit more awake now, she thought, *able to enjoy my annoyance to the fullest.*

Megan sat at the counter, doing her best to enjoy the scone and ignore the not-quite-right taste of the tea. Then she cleaned her dishes, stacked away the soup cans, and added several items to the family shopping list. Finally she headed back to her room.

Might as well warm up the computer, she thought. *See what I missed when I conked out so early yesterday evening.*

No sooner did she synch in, however, than she was confronted by a virtmail message, blinking the word UR-GENT at her. A little concerned, she called up the holo-text.

Exciting new discoveries have been made overnight in Latvinia, she read. *I hope you'll be linking in as soon as possible—*

Another one of Alan's not-so-subtle attempts to get

the kids to come out and play, she thought.

Megan was in the middle of erasing the text when her system announced an incoming call. *At this hour?* she thought, quickly moving to intercept the message before the system started waking up the household.

Alan Slaney's image appeared in the air before her. His hair was slightly mussed, and Megan could detect bags under his eyes.

"Did you get *any* sleep last night?" she asked.

He glanced away from the pickup—apparently at a clock. "Oh, man, I was just working. Didn't realize what time it was—sorry for calling at such an hour. When I saw that you were reading your virtmail—"

"You sent virtmail with strings on it?" Megan interrupted. It was technically feasible to send someone a message with a subapplication tacked on so that you'd know when the mail was being read. But it wasn't considered good Net manners—more the type of thing pushy salespeople and control freaks would do.

"I just thought you ought to know as soon as possible," Alan said apologetically. "One of Colonel Vojak's scouts came back. Princess Gwenda has been located."

"Where?" Megan asked, interested in spite of herself.

"She's in an old watchtower, converted into a hunting lodge," Alan replied. "Vojak and von Esbach are holding themselves in readiness. If you and your friend P.J. can link in, you can start making plans—"

Megan shook her head decisively. "Not now, and not for a while," she said. "If I go through another day like yesterday, I'll be of no use at fencing class tonight. You've seen me like that—I don't like it."

"It's just the planning," Alan cajoled. "You won't have to do anything—yet."

"Alan—," Megan rolled her eyes in exasperation.

"Not right now. No way am I going to roust P.J. out of bed at this hour for a planning session. Besides, I have things to do."

She glanced over at the shopping list. *Like getting a couple of quarts of milk in the house before my parents get up and then get cranky.*

"Maybe later, when you've finished?" Alan pressed.

Megan sighed. "Sure," she finally said.

Splashing water in his face, Leif looked in the bathroom mirror and grimaced at his bleary-eyed reflection. He stuck his tongue out at the image—

Yuck! It was coated with something!

No wonder his fencing connections—all early-rising, health-conscious types—had been giving him such concerned looks as he called them this morning.

They were all up with the lark, ready to go running, or do some other torturous conditioning exercises.

Leif, on the other hand, had gotten about two hours' worth of sleep. He'd synched in to the Net early in the evening, trying to talk to some of his less reputable friends up in New York. The result had been a virtual tour of some of the city's wilder night spots. But that's what he had to do to chase down some of these party animals. They played hard, ran wild—and simply loved gossip, the weirder the better.

The stories he'd collected from both sets of sources were . . . interesting, to say the least. They wouldn't appear in the news databases or police records his Net agents had scoured during his initial search for information.

But one thing was sure—the tales Leif had heard painted a very different picture of Alan Slaney from what he had seen.

Leif still had to verify these reports—he had enough personal experience to know that gossip rarely shrinks in the retelling. But his fencing connections had confirmed some of the stories. Even better, some of those friends had even given him numbers for people in the Association for Historical Fencing.

He took another look in the mirror and groaned. Maybe a shower and some cold compresses would be in order before he started cold-calling complete strangers.

Running a hand through his still-damp hair and clicking his now-clean tongue against his teeth, Leif cued-up his computer and began the calling process.

The first person he got hold of had been a student in the same salle where Alan had first gotten into historical fencing. She was a petite young woman with a slight foreign accent.

"Alain?" she said, giving his name the French pronunciation. "He was . . . brilliant. To watch him in the salle—he picked up every move as soon as Maitre Duchamps demonstrated it. And he listened, too. When the Maitre suggested a book, Alain went out to get it immediately."

She shook her head, short black hair flying around her like a halo. "Somehow, he even managed to get copies of rare fencing treatises from the seventeenth century." She smiled self-consciously. "He must have had lots of money."

"I sense a major *but* coming up," Leif said.

The young woman nodded. "He was very . . . impatient. Among historical fencers, you know, the more advanced students are expected to take the ones with less experience under their wing. Alain—he was so sarcastic—"

She bit her lip. "He mocked my fencing. And that was gentle, compared to what he did with some of the other, more clumsy ones. It was simply unacceptable. Finally Maitre Duchamps had to bar him from the salle."

Another call, and Leif got a young, muscular guy who looked more like a halfback than a fencer. "Slaney? Brilliant fencer. Knew his stuff, both academically and physically. Too bad the guy had a personality that made Atilla the Hun look like the king of mellow."

He shook his head at some sort of memory. "I got on his bad side—for what reason, I don't even remember. Anderson—you're the guy who won that junior championship? Yeah, saber."

Leif nodded.

"I compete, too," the guy said. "And you know how it is when you're bouting with someone you don't like? You put out a little extra effort to beat them. In saber, that means beating them up."

He ran his hands down the sides of his ribs. "Whenever I worked out with Slaney, I would be all black and blue. He would whale away at me, and I'd try to return the favor—but he had the edge on me. We ended up going corps-a-corps all the time. It was more like wrestling than fencing."

"What happened?" Leif wanted to know.

"Hey, I wasn't the only one getting the rough edge of Slaney's tongue—or blade," the beefy guy said. "In the end they canned him from the salle."

"I heard that," Leif said. "Maitre Duchamps—"

"Who?" the other guy said. "I'm talking about Santorelli's up on the West Side."

"Ooooooo-kay," Leif replied. "Guess I got that wrong."

• • •

Leif succeeded in catching a couple of other historical fencers before they set off for work. They also came from different salles, but they were unanimous about Alan Slaney—he was a primo S.O.B.—talented, but so nasty and overbearing that in the end the fencing masters in charge had to tell him he was no longer welcome.

By this point the office of the Association for Historical Fencing had opened. "Good morning," Leif said to the woman who answered the call. "I'm inquiring about the credentials of a member, Alan Slaney—"

"I'm sorry, sir. Mr. Slaney is *not* a member of the association."

Leif didn't have to fake his confusion. "I—I don't understand," he stammered. "I was given to understand Mr. Slaney received his training in New York and belonged—"

"He is a former member," the association's representative admitted.

"Is he terribly no good?" Leif asked. "How do you know he's out of the club? What did he do?"

"Mr. Slaney's case is unfortunately quite well-known to the administrators of the association," the woman said carefully. "His expulsion was not a case of academic knowledge or fencing ability." She looked uncomfortable. "It was a question of attitude. Members complained that his approach was incompatible with the aims and ideals of our group."

"So he was a real creep?" Leif said.

"Sir," the woman replied, "we do not comment on Alan Slaney."

David looked as though he'd been awake for some time when Leif called.

"Cartoon duty," he explained. "The little guys are

only allowed to watch so much holo entertainment. And I get to supervise—you know, make sure it doesn't get too intense for them. But one of their favorite shows is at the crack of dawn."

"Can't you just record it and play it back for them?" Leif asked.

From the look David gave him, this argument was obviously a sore spot. "But then, when they go out to play, the other kids will have seen it already." He shook his head. "I'm sure that's not what you called up to talk about. Have you dug up more dirt on Alan Slaney?"

"I've talked to some people up in New York," Leif replied. "From what they tell me, Slaney left town about two steps ahead of a lynch mob. The guy was such a pain in the butt that, despite a bias toward blades, his fencing partners figured shooting was too good for him."

"Not like the well-known, well-loved Alan Slaney we've encountered." David frowned in thought. "Well, there are some possibilities. Maybe he's had his identity stolen—"

"By an impostor who just happens to be an expert historical fencer," Leif said. "Stop yanking my chain, Gray."

"So I guess you're not going to buy the pod people theory, either," David said with a grin. "Have you checked how he traveled down here? I envision an airplane almost crashing, a near-death experience that made Slaney completely reevaluate his life—"

"You are bad," Leif accused. "Once you start, you won't stop. But I'm afraid we have to get a little more serious. Here's a guy who loves fencing, but makes such a nuisance of himself that he has to leave New York. He comes to Washington following his other big interest, politics, but can't even hold on to an internship."

David nodded. "He's got an advanced degree in political science, and he's dusting computers in some corporate backwater. If I had those credentials and that happened to me, I'd be pretty damned bitter."

"Instead, he goes around like the male version of Little Mary Sunshine," Leif said. "I don't think he's had some great spiritual conversion. The stuff we've seen him pull in Latvinia pretty well contradicts that scenario."

David raised his eyebrows. "I think you may have put your finger on a motive for why he changed his behavior."

Leif frowned in sheer confusion. "What are you talking about?"

"No, it's what *you* were just talking about," David replied. "Latvinia. Slaney put a lot of time and effort into creating it."

"His perfect universe, which can only exist in virtual reality," Leif scoffed.

"It may be his private world, but he wants other people in it," David pointed out. "So he hooks up with the appropriate local AHSO special interest group, and becomes a professional nice guy."

Leif slowly nodded. "Okay. But why?"

David shrugged. "It's like the old saying. You draw more flies with honey than with vinegar."

"I know that, thank you," Leif said irritably. "I mean, *why* does he have to have people in Latvinia? What does it prove? In what way could it possibly pay off for a pretty intolerant control freak?"

"You'd have to drill a hole in his head to get any sort of answer—" David broke off his words suddenly.

"What?" Leif leaned forward eagerly. "You just had another thought. Spill it."

"I thought of one other place where we might get answers," David unhappily admitted. "It's a stunt you or Megan might think of. Captain Winters would definitely disapprove."

"Slaney's computer system," Leif said in disbelief. "You're suggesting we hack into the guy's personal computer! I can't believe it! When do we start?"

17

It's not fair that I have to do this, Megan grumbled to herself as she walked to the nearest store to pick up milk, muffins, and other breakfast stuff. *The boys devoured it all. Why should I have to replace what they ate?*

Unfortunately, she also knew that if she didn't take care of it, the shopping probably wouldn't happen. Mom and Dad were both working against tight deadlines to finish books. Her brothers would be tearing out of the house on training runs or heading off to summer jobs. Everybody would be hungry.

So somebody had to get food. And by getting it now, she'd keep the peace at home in a way that would benefit everybody, even her. Still, she sighed as she lugged the bag of groceries home.

Megan got back just in time. Her father came into the

kitchen, apparently moving in slow motion. "Coffee," he said in a hoarse voice.

"Fine, Dad. Just sit down. You know you're all thumbs when you've been up late working." Megan got a filter—great, running low. Something else that needed buying. She wrote it down, then loaded the coffeemaker, and soon the room filled with the smell of brewing coffee. Dad inhaled gratefully. Megan wrinkled her nose. Everybody in the house was a coffee drinker—except for her.

The boys came thundering through, grabbing cups of coffee and things to eat. Dad sat quietly enjoying his first cup of the day. Then Mom padded in, wearing slippers and a robe. She poured herself a cup and sat down opposite her husband. "You got to bed late," she said. "How is the book going?"

"I'm getting there," Dad replied. "Just a few chapters to go. But I've got to hit the library. Last-minute research. How's your project coming along?"

"My editor is acting like a little kid who has to go to the bathroom," Mom replied with a smile. "I think I'll have the series done before any real . . . accidents."

While both her parents headed for their computers, Megan did the dishes, then went through the house, tidying up. In the living room, she found three books lying on a table—*The Illustrated History of the Machine Gun*, *The Lives of the Saints*, and *The Book of the Sword*.

Dad's research, she thought, though trying to fit three such unlikely titles together was as much of a mystery as the story her father was writing. Megan skimmed through the third book with some interest. *Maybe I'll read this later.*

Then, because it was still her turn, she started collecting dirty clothes for another round of the dreaded laundry. With seven people at home, there was even more than usual. She ran a bunch of loads through the washer and dryer, folded up the clean clothes, and delivered them to the appropriate rooms.

Her final load took Megan back to her own bedroom. She glanced from her watch to the computer-link couch. Then, dumping her fresh clothes on her bed, she sank back against the upholstery of the couch, synching in, giving orders to her computer.

Enough of being a housemaid, she thought. *Let's have some people around to pamper me for a while.*

She opened her eyes to find herself in that library/ study on the second floor of the palace, sitting in her familiar seat while the Graf von Esbach came through the door.

"Colonel Vojak and your Texan friend will join us soon." The prime minister took a deep breath. "If all goes well, this nightmare might be over soon."

Megan gave him an impish smile. "So, you consider working with me a nightmare."

"Never in a million years, dear lady," the normally unflappable von Esbach protested, flustered for the first time since Megan had met him. "But for the colonel and I have had to do our duties under a terrible strain—not to mention you and your friends."

I certainly won't mention Leif and David, Megan thought. *They* would *have to bail on us just before things got really interesting.*

Colonel Vojak came in, a tightly rolled sheaf of papers in his hand. He was followed a moment later by P.J. Farris, who exuded a decidedly cindery smell.

Vojak unrolled the papers, revealing a map and a sketch of a three-story stone tower. "Several of our scouts were set upon as they searched through Grauheim. Three have not returned. But one of our men spotted a young woman attempting to escape from here."

"Thank heavens he didn't recognize her as Princess Gwenda," von Esbach said.

Megan examined the sketch. "What is this place?"

"It was built as a watchtower more than five hundred years ago," Vojak explained. "Villagers from the whole area fled there for protection during an invasion. The invaders slaughtered all they caught outside the walls. To deal with those inside, the invaders cut down every tree in the area, creating a pile of wood taller than a man around the base of the tower."

He paused. "Then they set it on fire. The stone walls served as a gigantic chimney. Everyone within died."

"In the old tongue the place is called *Horiela Kula*— the Burnt Tower," von Esbach explained. "Needless to say, it has a bad reputation. Gray Piotr's grandfather rebuilt the tower as a hunting lodge. But while he was staying there, he went mad, killing all the servants."

"Sounds like a charming place," P.J. muttered.

"I regret to report that *Horiela Kula* is a strong place," Vojak replied. "Thick walls, a heavy door, and a guard at the top of the tower would see an attacking force long before it could reach the entrance, much less break in. We would need artillery, and I don't think there are enough horses in the world to bring guns up that slope."

"I don't doubt but that you're right," P.J. said, "in the normal course of things." He jerked a thumb toward the study window. "But we have the equivalent of forty horses sitting in the courtyard outside."

Megan leaned forward across the table as her friend went on.

"I was with the colonel when this information came

in," P.J said. "In between, I've been talking with the palace blacksmith. Suppose we rigged a ram on that Mercedes. . . ."

It was late afternoon when David showed up at the Andersons' Washington apartment. He and Leif had talked it out and finally agreed to make the hacking attempt from Leif's system. David was really only contributing his knowledge of creating sims. Leif was the one who had the software for cracking into other people's systems.

The building's concierge called upstairs to warn Leif that a guest was on the way. Leif was already standing in the open doorway when David got off the elevator.

"A little eager, aren't we?" David said as he followed Leif inside.

"We've got time," Leif said, leading the way into the living room. They sank into surprisingly comfortable Danish Retro furniture as Leif went on. "I had a little chat with Sergei Chernevsky. This famous fencing class begins around six, and ends about ten o'clock."

He glanced at his watch. "We could order something in before we get down to business. My dad called. He's going to be out most of the evening on another business dinner. We can bet he won't be home until after ten."

David nodded. "All right. We have a four-hour window of opportunity to get into Slaney's computer and get some idea of what he's up to."

"If it takes an hour to get in, I will personally eat my computer system—without salt," Leif said. "How much time will you need once we've hacked our way in?"

"Two hours should be sufficient," David replied. He handed Leif a datascrip that he took out of his pocket. "This is the toolkit I'll need once we're inside. Of course, how long the job takes will all depend on what we find."

"So, in the perfect universe, we'll have an hour's grace—more, because we're not counting Slaney's travel time to and from the salle—however much that may be."

"You mean you haven't been following him with a stopwatch?" David joked.

"I'm afraid I'm not that obsessive—unless it comes to food." The boys got up and headed into the kitchen, where Leif opened a drawer to reveal a stack of takeout menus. "What do you think?" he asked. "Pizza? Chinese? Mexican? Peruvian chicken? Good old American ribs? I think we've even got something from a Corteguayan place in here. . . . You decide while I load this into my system."

The rib place turned out to have more of a selection than David expected. But then, the Andersons were used to getting the best—even if it came to fried chicken. After two platters of specialties, fresh cole slaw, and surprisingly delicious roast potatoes, David was ready for anything—even a foray into a decidedly gray area of Net morality.

The boys decided not to synch into the Net, since that would mean connecting another computer-link couch into Leif's system. "I get headaches enough with just one couch in the circuit," Leif said.

David shrugged. "I'd be just as happy to keep one layer removed from what we're doing," he admitted.

They seated themselves facing the display of Leif's system, and Leif began giving orders. The holo display went foggy for a moment, then cleared to show the living room of Leif's virtual stave house. On the low table in front of the couch was a collection of small doodads.

They looked like misplaced game pieces—except for the unearthly glow around them.

"Looks like you were already sorting through your toys." David shot Leif a look. "Either that, or you didn't want me to see where they came from."

"A bit of both," Leif said, a bit shamefaced. Quickly he began describing the programs represented by the icons. "The jade ax is something called Cracker—it will get you into a system, but it may leave some damage along the way."

"So the victim will know he's been hacked," David said. "Do we want that?"

"It's the old trade-off—dependability versus subtlety. The electric-blue bundle of wires with a switch in the middle, that's Splice, version 122.5—very good if you're expecting a lot of alarms and stuff." He glanced at David. "Are we?"

"I wish I could say," David sighed. "The Alan we've been introduced to in public—"

"The Dr. Jekyll version," Leif put in.

David nodded. "He probably would just have an easily hacked password. But if he's actually hiding something—à la Mr. Hyde—he's probably got security up the wazoo."

"Tripwires, firewalls, encryption—and alarms," Leif agreed.

David pointed at what he considered the most disturbing of the icons on display. "What's that supposed to be? The sort of off-green amoeba thing." The icon had the sickly phosphorescence of rotting wood and kept changing shape, oozing along the surface of the table.

"That's Amorph," Leif replied.

David gave him a different sort of look. He'd read about Cracker and Splice. But Amorph was a new hacking weapon. "Is it as good as everyone says?"

"I haven't tried it yet," Leif admitted. "Just happened to pick it up recently."

"From what I hear, it sort of slurps around system defenses, infiltrating right into the security programming and opening things up. Sort of a trapdoor program, except it opens the front door for you."

Leif nodded. "All I can say is, it made my security look like Swiss cheese."

"That sounds good enough for me," David said definitely. "Any drawbacks?"

"It can be slow."

David made a "who cares?" gesture. "Hey, we've got an extra hour."

Leif insisted on waiting until it was six o'clock before they began their attack.

"You're sure he's gone?" David teased. "Just our luck, he'd come down with stomach flu and be using his system to watch a holo sitcom."

"Oh, he'll be gone, all right." Leif was grimly confident. "Alan's got a big deal going on tonight. Sergei told me all about it. Besides the fencing class, there's a whole bunch of Latvinia role-players going to the salle tonight, to see how this sword-fighting thing really works. Our pals von Esbach and Vojak will be in attendance—not to mention P.J. Farris."

"Full house." David laughed.

"And you can be sure Mr. Slaney will be there, right at center stage."

Off in the living room an antique clock chimed the hour. "It's time," Leif said.

A new set of orders to his computer, and they were out of his virtual workspace, bouncing almost at random through the Net. The idea, David knew, was to lay as confusing a trail as possible between this computer and wherever they were going to launch the hacking program. If their attempt to break in was noticed, it should be impossible to trace it back to here.

The images on the display seemed to spin and swoop, making David wish he hadn't been quite so enthusiastic at dinner. At last they stopped in a grayish blank space.

"This used to be long-term storage—coincidentally enough, it's in one of the computers in the building where Alan works," Leif announced with a grin.

"We're lucky he didn't decide to expand Latvinia and erase your little hidey-hole," David shot back.

"Anyway . . ." Leif gave a few more orders, and the Amorph blob popped into existence in the middle of the dust-gray floor. Looking at a piece of paper, Leif recited a long Net address string. The Amorph icon faded from sight.

"I won't ask how you got that," David said. "Now are you going to burn it, or eat it?"

"Let's leave it for later," Leif said, "when we know whether or not we get in there."

They sat in silence, watching the dead boring image of a drab, empty room. David yawned and stretched. He rocked back and forth in his seat, wondering if there was time for a bathroom break before Amorph opened the way up for them. He glanced over at Leif.

"I *told* you this program takes its time," Leif defended himself.

"I know," David said. "That's the difference between what you see on the holovids and reality. Now I'm just wondering if we're missing out on any good holo shows while we wait."

At long last a portal of sorts began constructing itself in the inactive storage space. The empty doorway was the same sickly greenish-white as the Amorph amoeba.

"Looks like we're in," Leif announced.

"My turn now," David said. He called up his virtual bag of tricks, and gave the order to proceed. Leif had already programmed his system to respond to David's voice commands. They went through the portal, and found themselves in a disturbingly familiar room. It was the study/library from the palace in Latvinia—just multiplied by about twenty times. There was a ton of stuff filed away in here.

"Good luck," Leif muttered.

David pretended not to hear. He began deploying his weapons—directory crunchers, an internal searchbot program, even a file-viewing utility—and set to work.

After a long while David leaned back, listening to his neck crack. The more he'd wormed his way through Slaney's system, the farther and farther he'd hunched forward. "What's our time look like?"

"You've been grinding away in there for about an hour and a half," Leif replied. "Amorph took about forty-five minutes to get us in. We've still got about two hours. What have you got?"

"Not much," David admitted unhappily. "I've found bits and pieces of the Latvinia program, but he's not running the sim from this system—it just doesn't have the juice."

"That's a good thing, isn't it?" Leif asked. "A simple-minded computer means less stuff to be found."

"Yes—and no," David replied. "I keep coming across archived information files—stuff that's been downloaded from the Net, compressed, and stuck in storage. It may all be garbage—handy tips on how to build your own world."

"We knew he'd been downloading a lot of stuff on

that," Leif agreed. "On the other hand, this archived stuff could turn out to be his private journals from the time he was eight."

David nodded. "It just takes time to uncompress files, read 'em, and make a decision about whether or not they're useful for our purposes. We could be pawing around until midnight."

"Or?" Leif asked.

"We could copy it all—download it, and then paw around in your space until midnight."

"Could we fit it in the corporate storage we—um—borrowed?" Leif asked.

David nodded.

"Okay. Let's do that. Then we can both paw."

The download went quickly enough. While that happened, David checked to make sure he'd left no traces of his presence. "We probably should cover our tracks. Otherwise, isn't Slaney going to notice that his security has been neutralized?"

"I'll take care of that," Leif said, "after you leave."

David pulled out, and Leif began issuing commands. The phosphorescent portal collapsed in on itself. "Now Amorph will just disentangle itself," Leif announced. "When it's through, we'll just have that shapeless little icon sitting on my shelf in my home space again." He gave another order, and a duplicate viewing station to the one Leif had set up for himself popped out of the wall. "That side okay for you?" he asked, pointing to it.

"Fine," David said. He plunged into the archives they'd acquired, bursting out one document from every folder. Then he hit one section that caught his interest. David decompressed document after document, growing more and more worried as he read. He was so immersed, he didn't even notice Leif come over and give him a shake. Then he realized his friend had been calling his name.

Leif peered at the holotext. "When I have to go that far to get someone's attention, it's usually because they've discovered a set of naughty image downloads," he teased. "I was just going to tell you that the Amorph icon turned up—we're out clean. But now I wonder what's gotten your attention." He wrinkled his nose. "All I've turned up is recipe files for creating more realistic sims."

"Yeah, there are a lot of those," David said, tearing himself away from the display. "This stuff is more theoretical . . . but a lot more worrisome. You know how hackers sometimes joke about forbidden subjects? That's what this stuff is: 'how-to' diagrams on circumventing safety protocols when creating an off-Net virtual reality. Programming tips on giving you absolute control of the virtual environment while in veeyar. Reports on experiments to disembody human intelligence and port it onto the Net—"

"The old 'ghost in the machine' thing, huh?" Leif looked slightly scornful. "That's like the old-time alchemists trying to turn lead into gold. As far as I know, nobody's ever succeeded."

"Yeah—what worries me, though, is seeing all this stuff archived in one place. Put it together, and you've got a guy who doesn't want to be a ghost in the machine. He wants to be the disembodied supreme being of his own little universe."

"The god of Latvinia," Leif finished, a worried expression coming over his features. "What happens to the beta-testers when he tries this transformation?"

"I don't know—but I don't like this file I've been reading. It comments on the possibility of disembodying one or more persons to come along essentially as sub-routines in this private universe."

"Who would agree to that?" Leif asked in disbelief.

"This stuff doesn't necessarily talk about bringing them along willingly," David replied. "It just discusses the need for random interaction in the new environment."

"Translated, even people with a god complex might get lonely once they've been reduced to electrons." He shook his head. "But this is plain science-fiction—no, fantasy."

"I wish that were true," David said. "Not many people know it, but there have been experiments in disembodiment. The results—well, the experiments themselves have been hushed up. But I don't think they could have been promising."

He turned troubled eyes to Leif. "Alan may be clever, but I don't think he's clever enough to pull this off. If the rumors are right, every researcher who has ever tried this has either ended up with severe neurological damage"—he hesitated—"or dead."

18

"Dead?" Are you sure?"

David nodded.

"But this is all just theory and rumors," Leif pointed out to David. "It could be dead-end research. A lot of people read about stuff and never do it. A friend of my dad got the plans for the Bell Jet Pack off the old Internet in the 1990s. Every time he upgrades to a new computer, that file has come along. He even talks about building the crazy thing—someday. My dad has a bet with me that he never will."

David was back looking at the contents of the folder, running very quickly through the holotext. "Did your father's friend actually order the parts for the jet pack?" he suddenly asked.

"Uh, no. It's never gone that far," Leif said.

"Because that's what Alan Slaney has done. I just

found the files. I wonder if he was getting bargains for buying components in bulk. I figure he's got about ten times as much stuff as he actually needs to disembody himself."

"Ten times?" Leif echoed, his face going pale. "I guess Megan never told you—or you just sort of tuned it out whenever she went on about her fencing. The salle where Slaney works—students don't just do physical workouts. They train on specialized computer couches. They've got a back room full of those computer-link couches, nonstandard types that instill reflex responses in the nerves and muscles."

David abruptly swung away from the display. "Any idea how many?" he asked.

"I don't know that Megan ever spelled it out." Leif's voice sounded hoarse as he forced those words though his suddenly tight throat. "But I wouldn't be surprised if it was somewhere around ten."

The holotext now ran on unheeded as David stared at Leif. "Please tell me that the person who does the maintenance on them isn't who I think it is."

"Oh, no," Leif said bitterly. "It's none other than our smiling maintenance man himself. Alan checks them out personally every time anybody uses one, as well as calibrating them and keeping them in working order." Icy hands seemed to have invaded Leif's stomach and chest, clutching the organs inside with a chilly grip. He found himself fighting for breath. "And tonight is the big demonstration. The salle will be full of Latvinia role-players—both the fencing students and the people who were invited to observe."

"A very select guest list," David said suddenly. "You notice *we* weren't invited."

"At the time I just thought Megan was PO'ed at us,"

Leif admitted. "But what if it was Slaney—oh, no! Tell me I'm wrong here. Do you think he's going to try something tonight?"

"He could have gimmicked all those couches so they're running, not into the Net, but into his own personal computer—programmed with a very personal reality." Leif could see David was struggling to keep calm as he described the situation. David was also failing. "No Net, no safeguards, and they'd all be helpless while he does whatever he thinks he needs to do to suck them permanently into the sim."

"Do you think a—I don't know what else to call it but a soul—could survive in cyberspace?" Leif asked.

"I can only repeat the rumors I've heard. No one has ever been contacted by any of the people who intentionally disembodied themselves," David said quietly. "Whatever happens, as far as we'd know, those people would be dead."

"The time!" Leif cried, glancing at his watch. "It's almost ten—the end of the class! Alan's demo is scheduled to start right afterward." He sprang to the computer, shouting orders that immediately cleared the display. "We've got to call Megan!" he said desperately. "We've got to get her out of there!"

Inside the salle Megan removed her mask and toweled her face dry. It had been a good evening, an interesting class and an especially long set of bouting sessions. She'd done well against people at her own level of skill, and even given a couple of more experienced fencers, including Sergei, a run for their money.

Turning to the bench running along one wall of the training area, she grinned at P.J. Farris.

"I begin to see why you and Leif enjoy this stuff so

much," P.J. said. "Part of it is like a deadly dance, but it's obvious you've got to think out every move."

Megan laughed. "Somebody once described it as full-contact chess."

"I also saw how good Alan is with those pig-stickers," P.J. went on. "We'll face an uphill fight if we've got to take him on in Latvinia hand-to-hand."

"All too true," the man sitting next to P.J. agreed. Megan looked at him, and her eyes went wide. Add about fifteen years, and a pair of big, fluffy sideburns—

"Joe Brodsky," the oddly familiar stranger said, shaking hands. "By day, a lowly worker in the Council for Public Policy. On lunch hours and by night, however, you know me as the Graf von Esbach." He laughed at himself. "Veeyar is about the only way I could hope to reach high political office."

He turned to the guy sitting beside him, a tight-faced, balding guy who looked as if he should have a monocle in place. The second man cracked a smile, however, and introduced himself. "Walt Jaeckel, formerly a Navy Shore Patrolman, now a postal investigator. Or if you prefer"—he clicked his heels together and bowed—"Colonel Vojak, at your service."

"So, what did you think of the show?" Megan asked.

"Made me jealous," Brodsky said. "I was a fencer in college. This was a lot more—graceful, I guess. Less bloodthirsty. Definitely a lot less arguing than I remember."

Jaekel nodded. "Not at all like the slugfests you see on the Olympic coverage—if you stay up till about 2:00 A.M."

Alan Slaney walked in front of the group. "Thanks, everyone, for coming to visit tonight," he said. Something was wrong. To Megan's eyes, his smile seemed a little too broad—and a little too pasted-on.

He's trying way too hard, she thought, taking in the bags under his eyes—they looked more like bruises. Poor guy must be running on caffeine.

"I have a suggestion," Alan went on. "All you guys are involved in the same part of the Latvinian adventure. Rather than doing the demo I'd talked about, since we're all here, why not finish up our current beta-test adventure in Latvinia in one mass session?"

"The practice simulators in the back room!" Megan exclaimed. "What a great idea!"

She turned to P.J., who shrugged.

"I've got nothing big going on in the morning," he said.

Jaeckel laughed. "Nothing ahead for me except another day at work. Besides, if we finish up, Alan may get some sleep tomorrow—and he won't badger us to come in and play."

Alan's lips tightened a little in reaction to that crack. Then he laughed. "Guess I'm guilty on that one, Walt. What do the rest of you say?"

It didn't take much more persuading to convince the others to join in. Alan led the way to the rear of the salle, heading for the room filled with practice equipment, fencing memorabilia, and the computer-link chairs.

"Everybody set?" Alan asked as Megan and the others reclined on their couches. She closed her eyes . . . and opened them to nearly complete darkness. This wasn't at all like her usual entrances to Latvinia. Megan bit her lips to keep from crying aloud at the claustrophobic feeling. Had something gone terribly wrong with her Net connection?

Then she realized her hands were clutching something. It was a steering wheel—the steering wheel of the Mercedes Simplex! Megan was crouched in the right-hand driver's seat. As her eyes adjusted and she keyed into the sounds around her, she could tell she was out-side, and that the night was dark, moonless. She could only see by the faint light of the stars. But she began to make out what was going on. A squad of men—big, burly cavalry troopers—was pushing the car into posi-tion.

She looked up and, silhouetted against the stars, saw the square bulk of the old watchtower.

"All right," P.J.'s voice whispered, "you've got 'er lined up."

He had to kneel to get the starting crank inserted, reaching under the metal ram they'd attached to the front of the car. It was a pointed chunk of steel that reminded Megan of snowplows she'd seen. Except of course, that it was a couple of feet above the ground.

"Ready?" P.J. whispered.

She set the ignition, and he began to crank.

Just one favor, Megan thought, as she silently pleaded with the Fates. *No backfires tonight.*

The flywheel began its muted rumble as figures piled into the rear of the car. The Graf von Esbach had insisted on joining them, as had Colonel Vojak. Sergei was on board as well. Behind them, ready to charge in once they'd dealt with the door, was a squadron of cavalry.

P.J. swung into the front seat. "Go, go, go, go!" he commanded in a tense whisper. Megan threw the car into gear, and the car shot into motion. They flew downhill, probably coming close to the forty-seven miles an hour the engine was rated for. Megan shifted again as they encountered the upward incline.

As long as I don't turn us over, she thought, fighting

to control the wheel as they bounced and shuddered up the rutted road.

The world ahead turned pitch-black as the bulk of the keep blotted out the stars. Then they hit the door, the weight of the car and the ram and the passengers combined, all at full speed. Iron-strapped wood shattered, and they were through the door and into the keep. The first floor of the tower had been turned into an impromptu dining hall. A pair of trestle tables had been set up, and some of the guards were still carousing by the light of flickering torches. Megan steered their improvised tank right into one of the tables. Some seated drinkers went flying, while other revelers dove for their weapons.

P.J. rose up behind the windshield, his twin Colts blazing away. Megan pulled out her pocket automatic and added to the fire. So did the others. Von Esbach and Sergei both used their big horse pistols. Vojak had a rifle and bayonet—"More used to it," he'd said.

By the time the cavalry came thundering in, many of the guards were down, and the rest were retreating for the stairs that led to the upper levels.

"Don't let them make a stand!" Vojak roared, leading his dismounted soldiers in a charge.

Megan tucked away her now-empty pistol and drew her saber. It was a hand-to-hand fight now, her side trying to drive back Gray Piotr's people before they could block the stairs.

Von Esbach held her back from plunging into the fray. "We still can't risk you," he said. So she was pushed toward the end of the column as Vojak and his troopers stabbed and hacked their way up the stairs. The second-floor landing became a massacre-ground for both sides. Gray Piotr's people were, after all, great swordsmen, and now they were recovering from the shock of the sneak attack.

Then a lone figure came down the stairs from the top floor of the tower—Gray Piotr himself.

"Surrender, traitor!" Vojak shouted. Rifle held high, he lunged with the bayonet.

"No!" Megan shouted, realizing Alan was unarmed.

All Alan did was raise a hand. Megan heard a muted crackle, then the boom of thunder as a bolt like lightning struck the colonel!

"We've got to call Captain Winters," David insisted as he and Leif sat in the back seat of the autocab. "This is a job for Net Force."

"It's the middle of the night. We'd get some automatic answering program. Besides, we don't have the time to tell him, much less convince him, before it's too late," Leif argued. "He'll want proof—and what can we offer him?"

"We have all those archives—" David began.

"All theory, unless you personally know Alan Slaney," Leif snapped. "And how are we going to explain where we got all this perfectly legal theoretical literature that's making us panic? 'Well, you see, Captain, we just happened to be inside the guy's computer. How did we get in? Was it a legal search? Er, ah . . . not exactly.' Right now we're the only real lawbreakers in this mess, even though we were careful not to leave any traces of evidence leading to us behind."

Leif shook his head. "Assuming we did manage to convince Winters to help us, he couldn't get a search warrant based on what we've got. Any court would toss the request out, which means Net Force would have its hands tied."

"Until Slaney actually uses his computer to kill someone, and the body's discovered," David said heavily.

"Exactly. I won't wait that long." The image of Megan lying helpless on a computer-link couch while Slaney did whatever he had planned to her just froze Leif's heart. "If we get into the salle and see something that's not right, then we can call in the cavalry. But first we've got to get there and see what gives. And, maybe, just maybe, we're wrong. I don't know about you, but that's what I'm praying we'll discover."

He glared out the cab window. What was all this traffic doing out at ten o'clock, blocking the roads?

Actually, he knew the traffic was only moderate for D.C. The cab was moving along at the speed limit. It was only Leif's sense of impending disaster urging him to go ever faster that made it seem like the cab was moving at a snail's pace.

They reached the salle; David dashed for the door while Leif ran a card down the credit slot to pay for the ride. He joined his friend to find David tugging fruitlessly at the door handle.

"Locked," David announced. Further inspection revealed that the locks were mechanical rather than electronic, and wouldn't respond to any tweaking they could try via the Net.

"There's got to be a back way in, a window—*something!*" Leif said.

The building was a leftover from the dangerous old days of Washington, when this neighborhood had been crime-ridden. The front windows had been bricked up. Leif ran around the block. An alleyway gave access to the rear of the building, where deliveries would be made. The door was solid metal, without even an exterior doorknob.

"If the whole place is sealed up, how do they breathe while they're working out?" Leif asked.

"There." David pointed to a ventilation system outlet far above their heads. "Metal grill, and then we'd have to get past the fan."

"Great," Leif muttered. They went back to the door, but it was sturdily built and stoutly locked.

"I don't suppose you have any lock-picking experience we could apply to the front door?" David said.

Leif shook his head.

"But what have we here?" David exclaimed, going farther along the rear of the building. The light back here was dim. Although there was a lamp fixture over the back door, it lacked a bulb. But Leif's eyes managed to pierce the dimness to see what David was looking at. A glint of light on glass somewhere on the second floor, located next to one of those old-fashioned metal exterior fire escapes.

"Give me a boost up," David said.

Leif helped his friend stand on his shoulders, then watched as he clambered up onto the balcony of the fire escape. David lowered the ladder strapped to the balcony, and Leif climbed up and stood beside him.

"It's a window—maybe for an office," David said, carefully feeling along the dirty glass. "And it seems to be slightly open. Let's see if we can improve upon that situation."

Gently pushing the window up, David began climbing through it into the darkness beyond. He was only half-way in when he knocked into something that fell with a clatter.

A second later Leif heard a muffled *whumppppfff!*— and a scream from David!

19

"What the hell do you think you're doing?" von Esbach demanded, shaken out of his usual suavity. Or rather, Joe Brodsky had been shaken out of his usual character. "This is supposed to be a *historical* simulation, even if it's a little romanticized. We're supposed to be doing Anthony Hope, not H. P. Lovecraft. When AHSO hears about this—"

"You're in *my* world now," Alan Slaney replied. "And you should be honored that I chose you."

"You've gone off the deep end, Slaney." That was definitely Joe Brodsky speaking, not the polished Graf von Esbach. "I'm out of here."

He concentrated for a moment, obviously giving computer orders. Then his eyes went wide. "You—"

Slaney raised his hand again, but von Esbach/Brodsky

proved remarkably spry, dropping to hug the ground as the lightning bolt crackled over him.

"There will be no leave-takings," Alan's voice took on a deeper, more oracular tone. "You entered this world through *my* portal. And you will embark on a new existence here."

Megan was scarcely listening. She was busy trying to bail out of this sim—and the program kept coming back "permission denied."

"We're not on the Net!" P.J.'s voice was a hoarse whisper in her ear.

Those couches in the salle—they must have been hooked up to a stand-alone system, Megan thought. "It really is Alan's world. We're stuck in here—"

She looked down at the blackened form of Colonel Vojak.

And Walt Jaeckel might really be dead!

Megan wanted to recoil in horror as Alan stretched out a pleading hand to her. "Why do you shrink back from me? Don't you realize the boon I offer you? You'll be my queen."

"But you'll be our god, is that it?" She had to force the first words past a dry throat. But the more she spoke, the angrier she became.

"I've created a place where you'll never age. Remember what Burton—who was a fencer as well as a poet— wrote in the *Kasidah*. 'Hardly we learn to wield the blade before the wrist grows stiff and cold.' That will never happen with us."

"As long as no one pulls the plug on the computers where you're playing out this fantasy," she shot back.

The expression on Slaney's face didn't change, but the air seemed to get about ten degrees colder. No, there was a change. Faintly, then stronger and stronger, radiance began streaming from Alan's face, from his hands—it even seemed to seep through his clothes from the skin beneath, turning the heavy gray garments to a glowing white.

"You called me a god, foolish woman," Slaney said in a rolling voice. "In the bounds of this universe, that's true enough. Let all kneel to me!"

All around them the surviving nonrole-playing characters fell to their knees. The players with free will glanced at each other—and then the silence was shattered by the crash of a pair of matched Colts.

The heavy slugs from P.J.'s pistols didn't even seem to disturb the folds of Alan's clothing. Megan wasn't sure if they were disintegrated on contact, or if they just passed through.

"Damn," P.J. said as his guns ran empty, "I *knew* I should have sprung for some silver bullets."

The rage on Slaney's glowing face was a fearsome thing to see. He turned on P.J., both arms raised.

"Those sweat stains don't help the godlike image," Megan called, edging back toward the stairs.

Slaney halted in mid-gesture, peering under his arms.

"Made ya look!" Megan called over her shoulder.

She'd already grabbed P.J. by the arm as she plunged down the stairs.

From the way he was sagging, David should have fallen from the windowsill. But he seemed to be caught somehow. He was gasping in pain, scratching fruitlessly at something in the darkness. "My leg!" he said hoarsely. "Caught my leg!"

Leif dashed over, intent on helping his friend. But when he tried to reach through the window, his hand encountered a rough, splintery barrier. He pushed against it gently, and David almost toppled over on top of him.

The other boy cried out again in pain when Leif reached out with both hands to grab him. "It hit me again."

"Hang on to my shoulder," Leif ordered. More carefully this time, he pushed at the invisible barrier.

No, not invisible. Just well camouflaged. It was a huge sheet of plywood, larger than the window opening and painted black. The bottom gave when he pushed against it, but there was more resistance the higher Leif reached.

"Nasty," he muttered. Then he said to David. "You want to get in or out?"

"Out—unless you know what just slammed into me," David replied.

"It's a deadfall—a simple but very effective mantrap," Leif said. "Just a big-ass sheet of three-quarter-inch plyboard with a couple of hinges along the top end. Pull the free end up until it's parallel with the floor, prop it up with a piece of black-painted two by four, and the trap is set. The whole thing is invisible in the dark. When you started coming through the window, you banged into the prop, which fell. Then the sheet swung down, to smash into you."

" 'Smash' is right," David groaned. "Now I know how the fly feels when the swatter comes swooping down."

"So?" Leif repeated. "Out or in?"

David leaned heavily on his shoulder for a moment, silent in thought. "In," he finally said. "Can't get any worse. And it's not as though I'll be able to run for it if things *do* get worse."

"Brace yourself against me," Leif warned. He pushed against the hinged sheet of plywood, loosening it from

David's leg. "If I keep holding this out of your way, can you swing your other leg up and around?"

"I can try," David said.

It was a slow, painful business, but David managed to turn round on the window ledge and slide down inside. Leif could hear the hiss of pain as his friend shook up his injured leg on landing.

Some of the pressure against Leif's hands suddenly lessened. "I've got it from down here." David said. "Do you have enough space to get in?"

Leif succeeded in squeezing through—at the cost of a couple of splinter-scratches. Once inside he and David let the deadfall swing flat against the wall. As Leif knelt over him, David leaned back against the wall. "Go on," he whispered. "I'll be no help—except for calling in the backup."

"Backup?" Leif echoed stupidly.

"Trying to get into this building may not be the most legal thing I've ever done," David said grimly. "But death traps aren't legal either, dammit. This is a case for the cops—*and* Net Force. I think Captain Winters will listen when I tell him where I am and what just happened to me."

Leif could hear his friend fumbling in the darkness. "I've got my wallet-phone," David reported. "And the captain's number is programmed in. Leif—go! Right now you're the only one who can keep Slaney from doing something stupid!"

That thought hit Leif almost as hard as the deadfall had hit David. He scrambled up in desperate haste, then forced himself to move slowly, deliberately. He pulled out a small pocket flashlight, checking for trip wires or other unpleasant surprises Slaney might have set up along the way.

He was lucky, or maybe the deadfall hadn't been Slaney's brainstorm. Anyway, Leif made it into the hallway without further incident. He walked down a hall and a flight of stairs. To his left, shadows deepened into the large open space that was the salle. Across the way was a closed door—but he could see a strip of light underneath.

Leif crept across the corridor and tested the knob. Unlocked. Taking a deep breath, he grabbed the knob and threw the door open. He almost recoiled at the sheer bizarreness of the sight inside. Nine of the computer-link training couches were occupied. Eight of the occupants seemed to be under some sort of terrible tension—they twitched and jerked as if they were fighting to regain consciousness—but failing.

The tenth couch had just about been gutted. Circuitry and wiring had been pulled out from under the upholstery—and attached to Alan Slaney.

The handsome young man had taken off his shirt. Electrical leads had been taped to various points around his torso, to his neck, and to his head. The spots he'd shaved in his hair gave him a particularly unnerving appearance. He looked like the villain of a low-budget horror-holo, just escaped from electroshock therapy.

"It's over, Slaney," Leif told him, coming forward. "I know what's going on. Net Force is on its way—"

Slaney seemed only half-aware of him. Alan flung out his empty hand as if he were hurling something at Leif. When nothing happened, then Alan began to pay more attention.

"Keep back," he slurred. "Can't stop me." Lurching to the wall, he yanked one of a pair of crossed swords from its place.

That was not a fencing blade, but the real thing. Leif

recognized an Austrian dueling saber when he saw one. He stopped his advance, casting a quick glance to the wall at his right. A pair of straight-bladed sabers hung there as decoration. Leif darted over, pulling one free.

The sword made a solid weight in his hand. Wilkinson steel, an old cavalry blade.

Alan brought up his saber in the en garde position. "*Allez!*" he called, mocking Leif with the starting command from his disastrous duel against the French master.

But Alan didn't take the prissy position of the French saber school. He took the in-your-face stance of a Spanish sabreur, hand on hip—and point aimed right at Leif's eyes.

Leif stayed with the more modern Hungarian guard—offensive-defensive—but his fist, too, rested on his hip. His point kept moving, evading any attempt Alan made to establish contact between their blades.

Sneering, Alan put his own point out. Leif smashed his blade against his opponent's, trying to beat Alan's blade out of line and get a cut at his wrist. Twice, and then a third time, Leif pressed this attack, forcing Alan to take a couple of steps away to put his point back in position.

Finally Slaney got annoyed. He parried, throwing a cut to Leif's face.

Now Leif had to shift quickly to the defensive.

This isn't like that virtual duel I had back in Latvinia. Alan isn't going for a wounding cut to show me who is boss, Leif thought. *He's going for a slice to the face or throat that will end this little duel—permanently.*

But Leif had learned a few new tricks, thanks to his Latvinian adventures. He parried Alan's blade and threw the attack back at him.

Alan made a circular parry on the right side of his

body and lashed back with a cut to the top of the head. Leif brought his point up, to deflect the head cut, then slashed backward, managing to land a slice on Alan's sword arm.

Not enough to stop him, Leif quickly realized. *But maybe I can goad him into a mistake.*

"First blood," he said with a smile.

Alan surged forward furiously, only to be brought up like a dog pulling against a leash. The wires attached to his body kept him tethered to the computer-link couch.

"Damn you!" Alan shouted. "I'll kill you! I'll kill you all!"

Megan nearly broke her virtual neck tumbling down the stone stairs with P.J. in tow. But their painful—if unorthodox—exit threw off Alan's aim with the thunderbolt. Still, as she sprawled on the floor below, Megan knew she had little chance of dodging the next blast.

But Alan didn't throw one. Instead, he flung himself to the side, nearly scaring the fertilizer out of poor Sergei, who stumbled back as Alan pawed at the empty air. Slaney paid no attention to the Russian boy. Instead, he swung away, assuming the *en garde* position—except he had no sword.

He perfectly pantomimed a series of feints, followed by a retreat and a ferocious attack. Megan and P.J. rose warily to their feet as the macabre exhibition went on.

Then Alan flinched, and a splotch of red appeared against the radiance of his garments, as if . . .

"He's been pinked!" Megan yelled in disbelief. "He's fighting somebody out there in the real world, and he's programmed his system to mirror real world movement and appearance!"

But Megan's outburst had an unintended side effect.

Alan's distracted eyes suddenly regained their focus on the virtual world as he hurtled toward the top of the stairs. "Damn you! I'll kill you!" he shrieked. "I'll kill you all!"

Was that aimed at me? Leif wondered. *Or is it aimed at the people trapped in veeyar? What if he tries to discorporate them now?* He thought their fight had kept Alan from concentrating on his horrible project. Now he had to make sure he kept up that distraction.

He threw himself forward, making a feinting attack, a high cut at Alan's left cheek. When Slaney responded with a parry, Leif went in low, wrapping as many wires as he could catch around his blade as if they were so many strands of spaghetti. With a twist of his wrist, he tore the electrodes free of Alan's body.

Inside Alan's veeyar kingdom the trapped players were nearly hammered to their knees by Alan Slaney's scream. Megan forced herself to look at him. Leprous gray spots appeared in the would-be god's shining glory. Skittering, formless blobs of energy flew off from his body, seemingly at random.

One of them hit a nonrole-playing character, frying him where he cowered. The real people in the sim milled in confusion. Alan was between them and the stairway—their only exit from this floor. Blobs of death flew all around them, but they were more afraid of trying to get past Slaney and perhaps calling his attention to them than they were of the flying energy.

P.J. grabbed Megan's arm—hard. "Now would be a good time to come up with some brilliant programming," he said. "Looks like he's weakened and distracted. If you could maybe crack his system—"

"I'll try," she said dubiously. "Do me a favor—if you can, make sure I don't get zapped while I'm wrestling with the computer."

She closed her eyes, calling up every computer command she'd ever heard of, trying to see just how much control she could wrest from the system. . . .

The good news, Leif hoped, was that right now Alan couldn't go through with his insane plan to disembody himself and the people trapped on the computer-link couches.

The bad news was that Alan, one of the best fencers anybody had ever seen, was frothing-at-the-mouth mad—and now he was free to come after Leif, sword in hand. Slaney launched a set of multiple moulinets, his blade lashing back and forth around Leif's body, the sword whistling as if it were hungry for blood.

All Leif could do was retreat, frantically parrying, trying to get out of the way of Alan's slashing attack.

Alan's next move really surprised him. Instead of a slash, Slaney tried a thrust. Leif's parry was an instant too slow. Steel slithered against steel as Alan's blade rode along Leif's, almost deflected away . . . almost. The tip dug in just below Leif's left shoulder joint, where the pectoral muscles help hold the arm in place.

Leif staggered back. *Must have caught in my shirt,* he thought. Then came the pain . . . and the warm, trickling sensation along his arm. *Good hit,* he thought grimly. *A bleeder.*

Worse, he had absolutely no way to stop the flow of blood at this moment. Leif's left hand couldn't reach the wound. Just trying to move his arm sent a red-hot spike of pain through his shoulder. His arm hung uselessly at his side. And if he stopped long enough to try and to stem the flow with his sword hand, he'd be dead.

Leif knew he couldn't last much longer. That wasn't just blood he was losing. His speed and strength were draining away in the crimson tide. It was just a question of what would happen first—whether he'd faint or get caught against the wall that loomed perilously close behind him. Either way, Alan was going to kill him.

Wheezing, trying not to scream with the pain of the movement, Leif managed to tuck his left hand into the waist of his jeans. His shirtsleeve was already sodden, and he could feel the wet stain spreading across his chest.

Alan was tiring, too, after his burst of manic energy. He drew back on guard, his blade down and slightly to the side—a direct invitation for Leif to return the favor with a lunge of his own.

It was tempting—a chance to attack, maybe Leif's last. But that would be playing Alan's game. And the consequences, Leif was sure, would be fatal.

He slammed into action, running on pure adrenalin and muscle memory. Leif started with a modern move—pure Hungarian saber technique. Crossing over in front of his opponent, he stepped in, beat Slaney's blade down, and then flung himself into a running attack. But it wasn't a *fleche*. Rather, it was the ancient fencing move that preceded the lunge—the *passata*.

As he flashed past Slaney, Leif recovered from smashing down on Alan's saber, bringing his own blade up and around, swinging from the wrist.

The stroke caught Alan in the throat, a deep slice ending under the hinge of his jaw. Alan turned, staring at Leif, clapping a hand to his neck.

It was already too late. That slash had opened the carotid artery. Blood spurted from between Alan's fingers. His swing round turned into a spiral fall as he dropped lifeless to the floor.

Leif staggered as his adrenalin rush faded. He could see Slaney lying there, one spot in focus while the rest of the world blurred and darkened. His saber suddenly seemed too heavy for his fingers to hold. It clattered to the floor. Then Leif's knees began to give way.

Hope David gets help here quickly, he thought as he dropped. *I'll feel really stupid if I managed to stop this guy, only to bleed to death. . . .*

Megan struggled to consciousness, her body quivering from exhaustion. The struggle to defeat Alan's crazy programming left her feeling as through she had literally wrung out her brain. She forced herself up on the computer couch with a shaky arm, fearing she'd have to confront the mad genius.

Instead, she found Alan lying facedown in a rapidly growing red pool. Blood, it looked like. And beyond him, toppling like a chopped-down tree, was Leif Anderson.

It took her overstrained brain a moment to connect the bloodstained saber falling from Leif's hand with the body on the floor. Then she saw the horrible red splotch smearing half of Leif's shirt as he fell.

Leif wondered if he were hallucinating when Megan suddenly appeared, grabbing him with quivering hands. "You fought Alan to save me," she said, sounding as woozy as Leif felt. "You—you—"

Abruptly she seemed to snap into focus, becoming the Megan he knew only too well. "You *idiot!*" she yelled at him. "I knew you never liked Alan—"

"With good reason," he panted.

Megan paid no attention. "So you insist on playing with swords, and getting stuck. . . . Testosterone poisoning."

As she spoke, she managed to pull Leif into a sitting position—surprisingly gently. "Coming here alone—"

"Didn't," Leif replied. "David's with me. He got hurt in the office."

Megan glared at him as she tore at his shirt, revealing the wound. "You got David hurt, too?"

"Trap nailed him in the leg—he's calling for help."

"Morons," she muttered in his ear as he sagged back against her. "Bozos." Clasping him in one arm, she placed her palm right over the puncture, pressing down with her other hand.

Direct pressure to stop the bleeding, Leif remembered fuzzily from Net Force Explorers first-aid demonstrations.

"Can't believe how stupid—how careless—" Megan continued to rail at him.

"Y'know," he managed. "If this were Latvinia, y'should be swooning over me."

Megan made a noise somewhere between a laugh and a sob. "Dream on, Anderson."

Slumped in the circle of Megan's arms, Leif let his head fall back against her shoulder, awaiting the arrival of the cops, Net Force, and soon, he hoped, an ambulance. He could already hear sirens.

It was going to be okay. His friends were all going to live through this. Even Leif was going to survive it, despite Alan's best efforts to kill him. And Winters would have to wait until Leif got glued back together to yell at him for what was undeniably the nastiest mess of Leif's life. *But,* Leif thought muzzily, *it was self defense—any good lawyer will have me out of trouble in*

*the time it takes to file the paperwork . . . and thankfully,
I can afford a good lawyer.* And, best of all, Megan's
arms felt surprisingly good around him.

Yeah, he thought, trying to keep a smile off his lips.
A guy can dream, can't he?

PENGUIN PUTNAM INC.
Online

Your Internet gateway to a virtual environment with hundreds of entertaining and enlightening books from Penguin Putnam Inc.

While you're there, get the latest buzz on the best authors and books around—

Tom Clancy, Patricia Cornwell, W.E.B. Griffin, Nora Roberts, William Gibson, Robin Cook, Brian Jacques, Catherine Coulter, Stephen King, Jacquelyn Mitchard, and many more!

Penguin Putnam Online is located at http://www.penguinputnam.com

PENGUIN PUTNAM NEWS

Every month you'll get an inside look at our upcoming books and new features on our site. This is an ongoing effort to provide you with the most up-to-date information about our books and authors.

Subscribe to Penguin Putnam News at http://www.penguinputnam.com/ClubPPI